THE NECKLACE AFFAIR
AND OTHER STORIES

ASHLEY GARDNER

JA / AG PUBLISHING

CONTENTS

THE NECKLACE AFFAIR

CHAPTER 1

On an evening in late March 1817, I climbed to the third floor of Lucius Grenville's Grosvenor Street house in search of peace, and found a lady weeping instead.

In the rooms below me, Grenville's latest revelry tinkled and grated, Grenville celebrating recovery from a near-fatal injury. The entire *haut ton* had turned up tonight, Lucius Grenville being the darling of society, the dandy all other dandies aspired to be. The famous Brummell had fled to the Continent, Alvanley grew stout, but Grenville reigned supreme. He was an epicure who knew how to avoid excess, a sensualist who could resist the temptations of sloth and lechery.

I'd enjoyed speaking to a few of my friends below, but the transparent way Grenville's sycophants tried to exploit my acquaintance with him soon grated on my patience. I decided to sit in Grenville's private room and read until the festivities died down.

I used my walking stick and the balustrade, hand-carved by an Italian cabinetmaker, to leverage myself up the stairs. My leg injury, given to me by French soldiers during the Peninsular War, did not affect me so much tonight as did the near gallon of port I had drunk. I could never afford what Grenville had in his cellars, so when he invited me to partake, I took enough to last.

Therefore, I was well past foxed when I at last emerged onto the third floor and sought the peace of Grenville's sitting room.

I found the lady in it, weeping.

She sat squarely under the scarlet tent that hung in the corner of the room, a souvenir from Grenville's travels in the east. The entire room was a monument to his journeys—ivory animals from the Indies reposed next to golden masks from Egypt, rocks bearing the imprint of ancient American animals held pride of place near hieroglyphic tablets from Persia.

The lady might have been pretty once, but too many years of rich food, late mornings, and childbirth had etched their memories onto her face and body. Her large bosom, stuffed into a satin bodice and reinforced with bands of lace, quivered with her misery.

I took two steps into the room, checked myself, and turned to go.

"Captain Lacey?"

I halted, bowed, and admitted to be he. I had no memory of who she was.

The woman swiped at her wet cheeks with a hand-kerchief so tiny she might as well not have bothered. "May I make so bold as to speak to you? Mr. Grenville said you might assist me."

Had he, indeed? Grenville was apt to volunteer my services, as I'd been of some use in solving problems that ran from innocuous misunderstandings all the way to violent murders.

I ought to have walked away then and there and not let myself be drawn into the whole sordid business. I was tired and quite drunk and had no reason to believe that I could help this sorrowful lady.

But her red-rimmed eyes were so pleading, her wretchedness so true, that I found myself giving her another bow and telling her to proceed.

"It is my maid, you see."

I braced myself for an outpouring of domestic troubles. My head started to pound, and I sank into the nearest comfortable chair.

"She is going to be hanged," the lady announced.

CHAPTER 2

*H*er blunt statement swept the fog from my brain. I sat up straight as several facts clicked into place.

"You are Lady Clifford," I said.

She nodded, dejected.

"I read of it in the newspaper this morning," I said. "Your maid has been accused of stealing a diamond necklace worth several thousand pounds." The maid was even now awaiting examination by the Bow Street magistrate.

Lady Clifford sat forward and clasped her doughy hands. "She did not take it, Captain. That horrible Bow Street Runner said so, but I know Waters would never have done such a thing. She's been with me for years. Why should she?"

I could think of a number of reasons why Waters should. Perhaps she saw the necklace as her means of escaping a life of servitude. Perhaps she had a lover who'd convinced her to steal the necklace for him. Perhaps she bore a secret hatred for her employer and had at last found a way to exact revenge.

I said none of these things to Lady Clifford.

"You see, Captain, I know quite well who stole my diamonds." Lady Clifford applied the tiny handkerchief once more. "It was that viper I nursed at my bosom. *She* took them."

I knew from gossip which viper she meant. Annabelle Dale, a gently born widow, had once been Lady Clifford's companion and dearest friend. Now the woman was Earl Clifford's mistress. Mrs. Dale still lived in the Clifford home and, from all accounts, continued to refer to Lady Clifford as her "adored Marguerite."

But all of London knew that Lord Clifford spent nights in Mrs. Dale's bed. They formed a curious ménage, with Mrs. Dale professing fierce attachment to her old friend Lady Clifford, and Lord Clifford paying duty to both mistress and wife.

"Do you have evidence that Mrs. Dale took it?" I asked.

"The Runner asked just the same. *He* could produce no evidence that Waters stole the necklace, yet he arrested her."

The arresting Runner had been my former sergeant, Milton Pomeroy, who had returned from Waterloo and managed to work his way into the elite body of investigators who answered to the Bow Street magistrate.

Pomeroy was far more interested in arresting a

culprit than in slow investigation. He was reasonably careful, because he'd not reap a reward for the arrest if he obtained no conviction. But getting someone to trial could be enough. Juries tended to believe that the person in the dock was guilty, and a maid stealing from an employer would make the gentlemen of the jury righteously angry.

However, I conceded that Lady Clifford would know a maid she'd lived with for years better than would Milton Pomeroy. Interest stirred beneath my port-laden state.

"As I understand the story," I said, "your maid was upstairs in your rooms the afternoon the necklace disappeared. Before you and your husband and Mrs. Dale went out for the day, the necklace was in place. Gone when you, Lady Clifford, returned home."

Her lip curled. "Likely Mrs. Dale was nowhere near Egyptian House as she claims. She could have come back and stolen it."

My injured leg gave a throb. I rose and paced toward the windows to loosen it, stopping in front of one of Grenville's curio shelves. According to the newspaper, the other Clifford servants had sworn that Mrs. Dale and Lord Clifford hadn't returned to the house all afternoon. "You want very much for Mrs. Dale to have stolen your necklace."

"Perhaps I do. What of it?"

I touched a piece of jade carved into the shape of a baboon. "You must know that however much you want Mrs. Dale to have taken it, someone else entirely might be guilty."

"Well, Waters is not."

I studied the jade. Thousands of years old, Grenville had told me. The carving was intricate and detailed, done with remarkable workmanship. I rested the delicate thing on my palm. "You might be wrong," I said. "Are you prepared to be?"

"Mr. Grenville promised you would help me," Lady Clifford said, tears in her voice. "Waters is a good girl. She doesn't deserve to be in a gaol cell with common criminals. Oh, I cannot bear to think what she is suffering."

She broke into another flood of weeping. Some ladies could cry daintily, even prettily, but not Lady Clifford. Her large body heaved, her sobs choked her, and she blew her nose with a snorting sound.

I set the miniature beast back on its shelf. Lady Clifford might be wrong that the solution was simple, but she was in genuine distress. The fact that some of this distress was pity for her poor maid made up my mind.

Lady Clifford sniffled again into the abused handkerchief. "Mr. Grenville said I could rely on you *utterly*."

The little baboon smiled at me, knowing I was caught. "Very well, my lady," I said. "I will see what I can do."

~

"I DID NOT EXACTLY SAY THAT," GRENVILLE protested.

I eyed him from the opposite seat in his splendid carriage. I had awakened with the very devil of a headache, but I felt slightly better this afternoon, thanks to the concoction that my landlady, Mrs. Beltan, had stirred for me upon seeing my state. Grenville had arrived at my rooms not long later, and now we rolled across London in pursuit of the truth.

In his suit of finest cashmere and expensive kid gloves, Grenville's slim form was a tailor's delight. I bought my clothes secondhand, though I had a coat from Grenville's tailor that he'd insisted on gifting to me when my best coat had been ruined on one of our adventures.

I said, "Lady Clifford strikes me as a woman who so much wishes a thing to be true, that it is true. To her. But this does not mean she is mistaken. If the maid did not steal the necklace, I have no wish to see her hang."

"Nor do I," Grenville said. "Her predicament played on my sympathy. Lady Clifford might have exploited that, but I sensed she genuinely cares for poor Waters." He gazed out at the tall houses of Piccadilly then back at me, a sparkle in his eyes I'd not seen since before he'd been injured. "So, my friend, we are off on another adventure. Where do we begin?"

"I should speak to Pomeroy," I said.

I imagined my old sergeant's dismay when I turned up to muck about in what he'd believed a straightforward arrest. "And I'd like to speak to the maid Waters if I can. And we can try to discover what became of the necklace—whether anyone purchased it, and from where, and trace backward from there, perhaps to the culprit."

Grenville grimaced and glanced again at the city rolling by outside. "A needle in a haystack I would say."

"Not necessarily." I had pondered this all night, at least, as far as my inebriation would let me. "A master thief would try to get the necklace to the Continent, to be reset and sold. In that case the necklace is gone forever, and the maid obviously did not escape with it. At most, she was an accomplice. As highly as Lady Clifford speaks of her, we cannot rule out the possibility that Waters was coerced by a lover to steal the jewels. A petty thief, on the other hand, might try to dispose of the necklace quickly, close to home, which means London. If I were the thief, I'd find a pawnbroker not much worried about where the merchandise came from, one who knew he could reset and sell the thing with no one being the wiser."

"Your knowledge of the criminal mind is astonishing," Grenville said.

I gave him a half smile. "Sergeant Pomeroy likes to tell me about it over a pint now and again. And Sir Gideon Derwent has worked to reform criminals most of his life. He's told me many interesting tales."

"Very well, then, a petty thief who seized an opportunity might sell it to a shady London pawnbroker. But what if you were Mrs. Dale? A gently born lady, who likely has no knowledge of unsavory pawnbrokers?"

I shrugged. "If she is the evil viper Lady Clifford paints her, she either passed it to a confederate to dispose of it for her, or she is hiding it to pin the blame on the maid and upset Lady Clifford."

"A dangerous proposition. Would Mrs. Dale risk hanging to gloat over her rival?"

"I have no idea," I said. "The ways of lady rivals are unknown to me. But if the maid or other servants stole the necklace, we will find it at a pawnbroker's."

"Yes, but which one?"

"We check them all," I said.

Grenville gave me a look of dismay. I had always wondered how Grenville would respond when my adventures turned into dogged work, but to his credit, he did not try to wriggle out of his offer to help. "It will take less time if we recruit Bartholomew and Matthias and divide the search."

"Some areas are more likely than others," I assured him. "Not every corner in London sports an unsavory pawnbroker. And the theft will be talked about. We might be able to pry loose some information, at the very least."

Grenville squared his shoulders, wincing a little because the wound he'd received during our last investigation still pained him. "Very well. I will change my boots and soldier on."

The carriage listed around the corner, and I braced my walking stick against the floor to steady myself. The handle was shaped like a the head of a goose and bore the inscription, *Captain G. Lacey, 1817.* A gift, and a fine one, and it gave me an idea.

"I know someone who does understand the ways of lady rivals," I said.

Grenville knew exactly whom I meant. He shot me a grin. "Ah, but will she help?"

"Who can say? She will either be interested or show me the door." Lady Breckenridge was nothing if not unpredictable.

"Her observations are usually directly on the mark," Grenville said. "I saw her last week at a garden party, where she told me that if I'd hurt myself during the Sudbury affair, it was my own fault for not taking proper care when it came to you. Any friend of Captain Lacey, she said, was bound to come to some kind of danger, and that I was a fool to take what you did lightly."

My fingers twitched on the walking stick. "Considering I almost got the poor woman roasted alive, that remark was almost kind."

"And probably true, with regard to me. I tend to believe myself untouchable."

I still hadn't quite recovered my guilt over the incident, though Grenville had cheerfully taken the entire blame himself.

"I will write to her," I said. "And discover whether she will condescend to see me. If she does not think it too dangerous to associate with me."

"She would be an excellent person to ask for the lady's point of view."

"I hesitate to mention it," I said. "But so would Marianne. She's been an actress for some time, so she'd have seen female rivalry, as well as, I'm sorry to say, petty theft."

Grenville's expression went still, even blank, which I'd come to learn was his way of stemming his anger.

Marianne Simmons, who had lived upstairs from me before Grenville had spirited her away to a fine house in Clarges Street, was a bit of a sore point between us.

Marianne, as poor as she was, did not like cages, no matter how luxurious, and she'd flown from Grenville's almost at once. I knew why, and the reason was a good one, but I suspected she'd not yet told Grenville. She'd softened toward him when he'd been injured, but I hadn't spoken to her since his recovery.

"I am afraid I've not seen much of Miss Simmons of late," Grenville said in a cold voice. "But please, do ask her advice if you think it would be helpful."

"I've not seen her either. I wondered if you had."

"Not since shortly after our return from Sudbury." His frown held frustration, anger, and concern.

"I would not worry about her. Marianne is resilient and will turn up when she feels it necessary."

"Indeed."

Grenville glanced out the window again, and though he'd never admit it, even under torture, I knew he was struggling to regain his composure. The closest we'd come to a permanent falling out had been over Marianne. He knew that I knew her secret, and that I had given her my word not to tell him. Grenville and I had made an agreement not to speak of the matter, but I knew it grated on him.

Grenville at last turned back to me, his lips tight but his equanimity restored. "I will obtain a map and ask Gautier about pawnbrokers," he said. "If we divide the task between us and Matthias and Bartholomew, we can make short work of the search. And while they put lists together, you and I shall take a repast. Anton is experimenting again, and I need someone to help me eat his creations. If he continues on this bent, I shall grow too stout for my clothes, and my reputation will be at an end."

The troubles of the very rich, I thought dryly. Not that I would refuse a lavish meal prepared by Anton, Grenville's French chef. My pride ran only so deep.

CHAPTER 3

*A*nton did not like us to talk about business while we dined, especially when he was in a creative mood, so I endured the lobster brioche, asparagus soup, squabs stuffed with mushrooms, and a large and tender sole drowning in butter to please him. After each dish, the chef hovered at Grenville's elbow to wait for his precise opinion and hear what might be improved.

To me it was all ambrosia, but Grenville thoughtfully tasted each dish then critiqued its texture, flavor, piquancy, and presentation. I simply ate, while Bartholomew and Matthias, Grenville's two large, Teutonic-looking footman, kept our glasses topped with finest hock. Being Grenville's friend had decided advantages.

Once the final dish—a chocolate soup—had been taken away, Grenville bade Matthias bring out the map of London. Mathias laid out the leaves of it on the table, and the four of us bent over it. I was always fascinated by maps and resisted tracing the route to my own street, Grimpen Lane, off Russel Street near Covent Garden.

I tapped the area that showed Bond Street, Hanover Square, Oxford Street, and north and east up into Marylebone. The necklace had been stolen from the Clifford house in Mayfair. The areas I'd indicated could be reached fairly quickly from there and were rife with small shops and pawnbrokers, though those in Bond Street were less likely to purchase a strand of diamonds tossed at them by a serving maid or known thief. But one never knew. A Bond Street merchant had only last year been arrested for selling stolen goods brought over from France and Italy.

Bartholomew and Matthias turned eager eyes to me as they received their assignments. The brothers enjoyed helping investigate these little problems, and I often envied them their exuberance. Bartholomew had become my valet-cum-errand runner in order to train himself to be a gentleman's gentleman, but while he now held himself above other footmen, including his own brother, he'd never forgo the chance to help on one of my inquiries.

Grenville provided the shillings for hackneys to each of us, and we went our separate ways, agreeing to meet at a coffee house in Pall Mall that evening.

Grenville had been given the Bond Street area, because the proprietors there knew him well. Grenville was a Bond Street shop owner's greatest treasure. Not only did he have exquisite taste, but he paid his bills.

Matthias and Bartholomew hastened north toward

Marylebone, and I turned to Conduit Street and Hanover Square.

I found that pawnbrokers were less willing to speak to me unless I made the pretense of wanting to purchase something. Questions were not welcome, and clients kept in confidence.

I let them infer that I shopped for a gift for a friend and had difficulty choosing. The proprietors thawed a bit as I looked over bracelets that had once adorned the wrists of debutants and earrings pawned by wealthy matrons. That the jewelry now lay in trays for me to pick over meant that they'd been sold to pay off the ladies' gaming debts. In a world in which highborn women had little to do but gamble and gossip, ruin lay very close to the surface.

I found earrings encrusted with tiny diamonds, emerald brooches, and strands of sleek pearls. One shop carried a comb made of ebony with a sprinkling of sapphires that made me imagine it against Lady Breckenridge's dark hair. I eyed it regretfully and longed to be deeper in pocket than I was.

Nowhere did I spy a strand of diamonds that matched the description Lady Clifford had given me.

North of St. George's, just off Hanover Square, I found a possible candidate in a dark and dusty little shop. When I professed to the short, gray-haired proprietor with a protruding belly that I was looking for just the right string of diamonds for my lady, he admitted to recently having purchased such a thing. I tried not to hope too much as he fetched it from the back room and laid it out for me on the counter that it was the necklace I sought.

The diamonds lay against a black velvet cloth like stars against the night. The necklace winked even in the dim light, brilliance in the drab shop.

"Beautiful," I said.

"At a fair price. Fifty guineas."

Too dear for me, but far too low for Lady Clifford's diamonds. Her husband had valued them at three thousand guineas, Lady Clifford had told me. Even if the proprietor suspected the necklace to be stolen, he'd likely try for a higher price than fifty.

"Who would part with such a lovely thing?" I asked him.

"A lady down on her luck. What lady, I did not ask. A servant brought it, a respectable-looking lady's maid. Sad, she was. It was a wrench for her mistress to let the necklace go, she said, but she had debts to pay. It happens, sir. The way of the world."

My heart beat faster. "An unhappy tale," I said.

The pawnbroker nodded. "Pretty little thing, the maid. Probably worried she'd lose her place if the mistress had pockets to let. Felt sorry for her. Gave her more than I should have by rights."

I decided to approach the thing head on. I looked the proprietor in the eye. "You must have heard that Countess Clifford had a diamond necklace stolen. Her lady's maid was arrested for the deed. Can you be certain that the lady's maid who brought this in was not the thief in question?"

The man did not blink. "I read the newspaper account, of course. But these are not Lady Clifford's diamonds, sir. I saw her ladyship's necklace once, and I'd not forget a piece like that. The Clifford necklace was set in Paris and is much larger, the diamonds more numerous. And see here." He lifted the strand and pointed to one of the stones. "Cut is not quite exact, is it?"

I peered at it. The diamond, as beautiful as it was, had been cut slightly askew, the facets not straight.

"Lady Clifford's would be of higher quality, that is a fact," the proprietor said. "This bauble was intended for lesser gentry; possibly a country squire had it made for his wife. This would never be fobbed off on Earl Clifford. And I assure you, sir, were someone to bring me Lady Clifford's necklace, I would send word to a magistrate at once."

He said this with a virtuous air. I could not be certain whether he truly would send for a magistrate, but I saw no guilt in his eyes, no nervousness of a man who had stolen goods hidden behind his counter. If he were a very good criminal, of course, he would have mastered hiding his complicity, but short of forcing him at sword point to prove he did not have the necklace, there was not much I could do.

I thanked the man and left his shop, which was the last on my list. I took a hackney to Pall Mall, rather short of information.

I found Grenville already there. He bade the host bring us both a cup of rich, almost chocolaty, coffee while we waited for the footmen.

Grenville had found out little himself. The Bond Street proprietors had opened up to him, had readily talked of Lady Clifford's necklace, which was beautiful, they said, but they had no idea what had become of it.

"The task is a bit more difficult than I expected," Grenville said glumly. "The thing might already be cut up and in Paris."

I had to agree. When Bartholomew and Matthias arrived, however, the blond, blue-eyed brothers were pink-faced and grinning.

"Matthias has got it, sir," Bartholomew said. He dragged a straight-backed chair from another table and straddled it back to front. "Clear as day. In a pawnbroker's near Manchester Square. One large diamond necklace, brought in not three afternoons ago."

Grenville leaned forward, excited, but I tried to keep my skepticism in place. Though I hoped we'd found an easy end to the problem, I had learned from experience that solutions did not come so readily.

We had to wait until the publican had thunked down two glasses of good, dark ale for the brothers and retreated. Matthias and Bartholomew both drank deeply, thirsty from their search, then Matthias began.

"'Twas not much of a shop," he said, wiping his mouth. "It's in a little turning full of horse dung and trash. I told the proprietor that my master was looking for something nice for his lady and sent me to scout, but I didn't mention who my master was, of course. Would have swooned if I'd told him, wouldn't he? That someone like Mr. Grenville would even think to soil his boots in such a place would have him so agitated he wouldn't be able to speak. So I kept quiet, and he came over quite chatty."

"Good thinking," I said, as Matthias paused to drink.

"What he had in the front was mostly cheap,"

Matthias continued. "The sort of thing I'd expect him to show gentlemen of not much means. I said that my master was looking for something better, because he'd just become flush in cash and wanted to please his lady. Well, as soon as I said that, the proprietor came over all secretive. He shut the door of the shop and drew the curtain, and told me he had something special. Something he was keeping for customers who were obviously up in the world."

"And did he show it to you?" Grenville asked.

"That he did, sir. He brought out a necklace. My eyes nearly popped when I saw it. Lots of stones all sparkling. Much nicer than anything in that shop. Out of place, like. I professed my doubts, saying my master wouldn't have truck with anything stolen. Proprietor grew angry, said he'd never buy from thieves. If a highborn lady wanted to bring her necklace to a pawnbroker's, why should he mind? He paid her a sum which near ruined him, he said, and would be glad to get it off his hands."

I exchanged a look with Grenville. "A highborn lady," I said. "Not her maid?"

"Highborn lady," Matthias repeated. "I couldn't ask him for a description, because he was already getting suspicious of me. So I thought I'd nip off and tell you."

Grenville snatched up his gloves. "Well, if this pawnbroker is anxious to have it taken off his hands, we will oblige him. You've done well, Matthias. Lacey, come with me?"

I went out with him to his sumptuous carriage, and the two footmen pushed aside their ales and followed, not about to let us finish the problem without them.

When we reached Manchester Square, Grenville was set to leap down and charge into the shop, but I persuaded him to let me have a look at the necklace myself. Matthias was correct—if the grand Grenville walked into a down-at-heel pawnbroker's, the news would fly around London and be picked up by every newspaper in the land. I, on the other hand, in my worn breeches and square-toed boots, could enter any shop I pleased without all of society falling into a swoon.

Grenville was disappointed, but he conceded that we needed to go carefully, and said he'd wait in the carriage around the corner.

I had little difficulty persuading the proprietor to show me the necklace. It was much as Lady Clifford described it—a large stone with three smaller diamonds on either side of it, all linked by a gold chain. When I'd asked Lady Clifford for more particulars, she'd looked blank, as though she could not remember anything else about it. I wondered what it must be like to have so many expensive baubles that the details of them blurred in the memory.

I played my part as an ingenuous husband, recently come into some money, wishing to ingratiate myself with my wife. The proprietor volunteered that these were the goods, from a lady, in fact. A true lady, well-spoken and well dressed, not a lackey or a tart. I suppose Matthias had made him nervous with his questions, because the proprietor was happy to tell me all.

Grenville had supplied the money with which to purchase the necklace if necessary. I paid it over and returned to the carriage with the diamonds in my pocket, the pawnbroker happy to see the necklace go.

Satisfied that we'd found it, Grenville was ready to call on Clifford and confront Annabelle Dale on the moment. I persuaded him to fix an appointment for the next day, saying I wanted to be certain of a thing or two before then.

Grenville chafed with impatience, but he'd come to trust my judgment. I gave him the necklace to lock up in his house for the night, and we parted ways.

Once Grenville was gone, Matthias with him, I told Bartholomew to fetch us a hackney, then I returned to the shop near Hanover Square. There, I talked the proprietor down to a price I could afford and took the smaller necklace home with me. Bartholomew was full of questions, but I could only tell him that I did not know the answer to them myself.

The next morning, I received a note from Grenville that fixed a visit to the Clifford house in South Audley Street for three o'clock that afternoon. Lady Brecken-ridge, to whom I'd written the previous day, sent me a short and formal reply, as well, also giving me leave to call on her near three.

I had Bartholomew clean and brush my coat, and I left my rooms in plenty of time to hire a hackney to Mayfair.

As I walked toward Russel Street, however, a large carriage rolled up to block the entrance to tiny Grimpen Lane, where my rooms above the bake shop lay. Grimpen Lane was a cul-de-sac, no other way out. I halted in annoyance.

I knew to whom the coach belonged, which

annoyed me further. I did not at the moment want to speak to him, but I was unable to do anything but wait to see what he wanted.

A giant of a man stepped off his perch on the back of the coach and opened the door for me. He assisted me in, slamming the door as I dropped into a seat, leaving me alone to face James Denis.

Denis was a man who had his hand in most criminal pies in England, who obtained precious artworks —the ownership of which was hazy—from half-wrecked Europe, and bought and sold favors of the highest of the high. He owned MPs outright, and with a flick of his well-manicured fingers, had them manipulate the laws of England to suit him. London magistrates, with only two exceptions that I knew of, answered to him. Denis had the power to ruin many without a drop of that ruin touching him.

I thoroughly disliked what Denis was and what he did, but I was not certain how I felt about the man himself. I'd never, in the year I'd known him, gotten past his façade. He was so thoroughly cold and revealed so little of himself that anyone could reside behind that slim, rather long face and dark blue eyes. Denis was only in his thirties, and I had to wonder what on earth had happened to him in his short life that had made him what he was.

The carriage remained squarely in front of the entrance to Grimpen Lane, and I knew it would remain there until Denis had gotten from me what he wanted.

"The Clifford necklace," he said without greeting me. "You've undertaken to find it."

He did not ask a question. That he already knew

about my involvement did not surprise me. He paid people in my neighborhood to watch me and report to him everything I did.

I saw no benefit in lying. "I have. What is your interest?"

"Let us say I have had my eye on the piece. I would very much like to be informed when you have found it."

"Why?" I asked, curious in spite of myself. "It is a Mayfair lady's necklace. Expensive, yes, but hardly in your league."

His expression did not change. "Nevertheless, report to me when you have found it. Better still, bring it to me."

I regarded him as coolly as he regarded me. "I know you find this repeated declaration tedious, but I do not work for you. Nor do I ever intend to work for you. Lady Clifford asked me to discover what has become of her necklace, and that is what I will do."

Denis did not like the answer *no*. He'd been known to punish—thoroughly and finally—those who told him no too often. But I could not say anything else. I had pledged myself to Lady Clifford, and that was that.

"I did not say I would not allow you to return the diamonds to Lady Clifford," Denis said. "I want to examine the necklace myself first, is all."

"Why?"

"That, Captain, is my business."

Meaning I'd never drag the reason out of him, no matter how much I tried. "What is special about this necklace?" I asked instead. "You betray yourself with too much interest."

Denis tapped his walking stick on the roof and almost instantly, the pugilist footman wrenched open the door. "That I can determine only when I hold it in my hands. Good day, Captain."

The footman helped me climb to the ground. Denis turned to look out the opposite window as the footman closed the door again, finished with me.

I was happy to go, but he'd started me wondering. Denis did not involve himself in anything that did not bring him great profit. A missing lady's necklace should be, as I'd told him, far below his notice. I would have to find out.

The carriage rolled on, unblocking the lane, and I continued on my way to the hackney stand.

Once I reached Grenville's house in Grosvenor Street, we rode in his carriage to our appointment with Lord Clifford.

Lord Clifford's study, where he received us, was crammed with books up to its high ceiling, the tall windows letting in light. I saw no dust anywhere, but the place smelled musty, as though damp had gotten into the books.

Lord Clifford was a tall man with a bull-like neck and small eyes. He wore clothes that rivaled Grenville's for elegance, but he looked more like a farmer in his landlord's clothes than a gentleman of Mayfair.

"Lot of nonsense," Clifford said to us after Grenville introduced me and told him our purpose. "Waters never took the blasted necklace. I told the magistrate so, and he released her. She is home, safe and sound, back below stairs, where she belongs."

CHAPTER 4

*G*renville and I stared at him, dumbfounded.

"You made your inquiries for nothing, gentlemen," Lord Clifford said. "All I had to do was have words with the magistrate. If my wife hadn't gone ranting to all and sundry that the necklace had been stolen, her maid would not have been arrested at all. Serves her right for not leaving me to deal with it. Some housebreaker took it, must have done. The Runner had it all wrong."

"I would not say our inquiries were for nothing," I began.

Clifford gave me a look that told me I should not speak before my betters. "Of course they were. I told you. The bloody thing's probably on the Continent by now. Long gone."

"What the captain means is that we may have found your necklace," Grenville said. He removed a box from his pocket and opened it to reveal the necklace Matthias had run to ground yesterday.

The earl stared at it. "Who the devil gave you this?"

"I purchased it from a pawnbroker near Manchester Square," Grenville answered.

Clifford studied the diamonds a moment, then he snorted. "Well, he played you false, then. This is not my wife's necklace."

Grenville blinked, but for some reason, I felt no surprise.

"Are you certain?" Grenville asked.

"Of course I am certain. I gave her the damned thing, didn't I? My diamonds were of much finer quality and more numerous, the smaller stones surrounded by even smaller ones. I've never seen this necklace before."

I dipped into my pocket and removed the strand I'd persuaded the proprietor off Hanover Square to sell me last evening. "What about this one?"

Grenville shot me a look as Lord Clifford examined the stones. "Yes, this belongs to my wife. But it is not the necklace that was stolen. She's had this since before we married. Bit of trash." He tossed the necklace onto a satinwood table and did not ask me where I'd obtained it. "Someone has played you for a fool, Grenville. Probably my wife. She is eaten up with jealousy. Her maid never stole the necklace, and neither did Mrs. Dale, as much as she's putting that story about."

"Can you be certain about Mrs. Dale?" I asked.

"Mrs. Dale was with me at the time the necklace disappeared." Lord Clifford touched the side of his nose. "You gentlemen understand what I mean."

Grenville looked pained. "Quite."

"So," I said, "not at Egyptian House, as she told the Runner."

"Well, of course not, but she could hardly confess where she truly was, could she?" Lord Clifford jerked his thumb at the necklace in Grenville's hand. "Enjoy the bauble, gentlemen. You bought it for nothing. Teach you to go mucking about in a man's affairs. Should be ashamed of yourself, Grenville."

He made no such admonishment to me—whether because he expected someone like me to not know any better or because he caught the angry look in my eye, I didn't know. Grenville, his sangfroid in place, bade Clifford a cool good afternoon, and we took our leave.

The sangfroid slipped, however, as the carriage pulled away from Lord Clifford's door. "Boor," Grenville said between his teeth. "I've never liked him." He transferred his annoyed stare to me. "Where did you find that other necklace? Why did you not tell me about it?"

"Because I was not certain," I said. "It was a pure guess, and I could have been entirely off the mark."

"Bloody hell, Lacey, you do play your cards close to your chest. What is this all about?"

"I am not sure, truth to tell. Lady Clifford sells one necklace and has the other stolen, or so she claims. Too much coincidence."

Grenville heaved a sigh. "At least the maid has been cleared. Perhaps Lady Clifford only harangued about the necklace being stolen to push the blame onto Mrs. Dale. For vengeance. Then feels remorse when her beloved maid was accused instead and turned to you to unravel the tangle."

"I do not think it is quite so simple." I thought of Lord Clifford throwing aside the necklace I'd bought, proclaiming it a "bit of trash." He'd not even asked where I'd found it or why I'd had it. "But I am happy the maid was allowed home."

"And what has the second necklace to do with anything?"

"I am not certain. I need to think on it."

Grenville put the pouch containing the wrong necklace we'd bought into his pocket. "I suppose I can find a use for this," he said.

I doubted he meant to give it to Marianne. He'd buy her something new, something another woman hadn't already worn. Marianne might not appreciate it, but Grenville treated her better than she deserved.

"Can you ask your coachman to let me out here?" I asked, glancing out the window. "Lady Breckenridge answered my request to call on her, and her house is only a few doors down."

I knew Grenville was irritated with me, but he agreed. As I descended at Lady Breckenridge's door, Grenville gave me a pointed look. "We will speak later."

Which meant I would have to confess everything. I tipped my hat to him, he muttered a goodbye, and the carriage rolled away.

LADY BRECKENRIDGE, COOL IN A GRAY SO LIGHT IT was silver, her dark hair threaded with a wide bandeau, regarded me from beside the fireplace in her very modern drawing room.

I'd sat in this drawing room amongst the highest of the high a few weeks ago, when the double doors between this chamber and the next had been pulled open, the room filled with chairs and people. We'd listened to a tenor make his London debut, and while I'd not thought much of the young man as a person, his voice had filled me with joy.

The drawing room had been restored to its former arrangement of sofas and chairs, footstools and side tables, grouped together under a chandelier dripping with crystals. The chandelier was dark today, the room illuminated by sunlight streaming through the two front windows.

Lady Breckenridge did not sit down, so I remained standing.

"Business, your letter indicated," she said.

"Indeed," I said. "I thank you for agreeing to admit me."

She lifted one dark brow. "Gracious, Lacey, your conversation has become as stilted as your letters. I had half a mind to ignore your request on that transgression alone."

The note I'd dashed off to her yesterday afternoon, written on a scrap of paper I'd torn from a letter she'd sent me during my sojourn in Sudbury, had requested a half hour of her time and said nothing more. I suppose it had been a bit abrupt.

"Forgive me," I said, giving her a half bow. "I ran away to the army before I was able to complete my upbringing and learn the gentlemanly art of entertaining letters. I was in a hurry."

Lady Breckenridge did not smile. "It was not so much the form of the letter, you know, as the request within it. If you wish to see me only in a matter of business, I hire gentlemen to take care of that for me. I can give you their direction."

I'd offended her, I realized. Not long ago, in this very drawing room, I'd told her that I counted her among my circle of close friends, of which I had few. I realized that my hasty missive yesterday must have seemed brusque, demanding, and nothing to do with friendship.

"I beg your pardon," I said, giving her another bow. "Grenville admonishes me in much the same way. I get the bit between my teeth, and I forget that I am easily rude. I said 'business' because I hate to take advantage of friendship, and I find myself needing your help."

Her dark blue eyes remained cool. "Ah, you thought yourself softening the blow. I must say, you do not read your fellow creatures well."

"I never pretended to."

Lady Breckenridge regarded me a moment longer, then she uncrossed her arms, moved to a settee near the fireplace, and reposed gracefully on it. She sat in the middle, so if I tried to join her, I'd either crush against her or force her to move.

I chose a chair instead, one near enough to her to be conversational but not so close as to impose myself.

Lady Breckenridge was not a woman who flirted or was coy, and she did not like coyness in return. She asked for honesty and was somewhat brutally honest herself. Her marriage had been unhappy, her husband a bully. I suppose she had taught herself to trust cautiously.

"Well, then, what is this business?" Lady Breckenridge asked. "If it is entertaining enough, I might consider forgiving you both the letter and the presumption."

"It's to do with Lady Clifford's stolen necklace."

Lady Breckenridge stopped short of rolling her eyes. "Good God, I am bloody tired of hearing about Lady Clifford and her bloody necklace. The woman has a flair for the dramatic, always making heavy weather of something—her husband, her daughter's marriage, the hated Mrs. Dale, her losses at cards, her stolen necklace. If you ask me, she sold the damned thing to pay her creditors and professed it stolen so that her husband would not discover she is up to her ears in debt."

"I wondered if she might game deeply," I said.

"She has a mania for it. Sometimes she wins, mostly she loses. Lord Clifford has come to her rescue before, but I gather he has made it clear that she is to cease. Not that she has."

I thought about the smaller necklace Lord Clifford had sneered over, declaring it one his wife had owned before their marriage. The pawnbroker had told me that a lady's maid had brought it in for her mistress who was "down on her luck." Lady Clifford selling her own jewelry to get out of debt explained the transaction, but Lady Clifford hadn't claimed *that* necklace to be stolen.

"Grenville and I and our footmen searched every

jeweler's and pawnbroker's up and down the center of London," I said. "If Lady Clifford had sold the necklace, surely we would have found it, or at least heard word of it." As I had with the smaller necklace.

"My dear Lacey, if I wanted to sell my diamonds and pretend them stolen from me, I wouldn't rush to flog it to a pawnbroker. I'd be much more discreet. There are gentlemen who do that sort of thing for you."

"What sort of men?" I asked. I'd not heard this, but then I was not much of a card player. I preferred more active games of skill—billiards, boxing, horseracing.

"Oh, one can find them if one knows where to go," Lady Breckenridge said, looking wise. "Who, for a percentage, are willing to smuggle bits and pieces out of the country while you go on a tear about having them stolen. You pay off your creditors, your husband or wife or father never knows, and embarrassment is saved all around."

"She might have done such a thing, true. But why then loudly point at Mrs. Dale? Lord Clifford tells me that Mrs. Dale was—shall we say, entertaining him— at the time the necklace went missing. Mrs. Dale would have to reveal that alibi to save herself, possibly in a public courtroom. The world knows that Lord Clifford is carrying on with his wife's companion, but would Lady Clifford wish to publicly acknowledge it?"

"Lady Clifford rather enjoys playing the wronged woman, I think," Lady Breckenridge said. "Much sympathy flows her way, though much disgust as well, I am afraid. The way of the world is such that when a man is unfaithful to his wife, it of course must be because the wife has not done enough to keep him at her side."

I heard the bitterness in her voice. Lady Breckenridge's late husband had been notorious for straying. While Lady Breckenridge had professed she'd been rather grateful for his habit, because it kept the boorish man away from her, I imagined that she'd faced blame the likes of which she'd just related. Hardly her fault that her husband had been cruel and uncaring.

"I am sorry," I said.

"I did not say such a thing to stir your sympathy, Captain. It is only the truth."

I knew that when my wife had left me, no one had blamed me harder than I had myself. I'd blamed Carlotta as well, yes, in my rage and heartbreak. I could have behaved better toward her, but she ought to have told me how unhappy she'd been. And I'd never forgiven her for taking away my child. My girl would be quite grown now. I hadn't seen her in fifteen years.

The last thought hurt, and for a moment, there in Lady Breckenridge's sitting room, the pain of it squeezed me hard. I studied the head of my walking stick, the one Lady Breckenridge had given me, as I fought to regain my composure.

"Captain?" she asked. "Are you well?"

Her voice was like cool water in the darkness. I looked up to find Lady Breckenridge watching me, her arms stretched across the back of the settee now, which made her more graceful and lovely than ever. The pose was practiced, probably trained into her by a ream of governesses and her aristocratic mother.

"I beg your pardon," I said.

Any other lady might express curiosity about my thoughts and why I'd let my attention stray from her, but not Lady Breckenridge.

"You have not told me precisely why you need my help," she said.

I did not know quite how to begin. This was the first investigation in which I'd found a place I could not go, people I could not question. I was generally accepted among Grenville's circle if not embraced, because my pedigree measured up even to the most snobbish. Additionally, because I took rooms over a bake shop in a genteelly poor section of town, I was able to speak to the denizens of Covent Garden and beyond without awkwardness. But an aristocratic lady's private rooms were beyond my sphere, and I doubted Lord Clifford would invite me to return his house, in any case.

"Say it all at once, and I shall respond," Lady Breckenridge said. She sounded in no hurry.

"Lady Clifford's maid was released, absolved of the crime," I said. "But I know Pomeroy. He will harass the household until he finds another culprit to take to trial—a footman, another maid, even Mrs. Dale. I'd like to find the true culprit, and the necklace, before that happens. To do so, I will better need to know the layout of the Clifford house and what happened on the day of the theft. Unfortunately, Lord Clifford has made it clear that I am unwelcome, and I have no idea when I will be able to speak to Lady Clifford again."

"I see," she said after a thoughtful moment. "And so you thought to ask me to speak to her for you."

I could not tell whether she were pleased at the

prospect or dismayed. Her tone was neutral, her look direct.

"Discreetly," I said.

"By all means, discreetly. It would have to be. Lady Clifford and I don't exactly see eye to eye. Not a pleasant task you thought to set me."

"You see now why I did not want to presume upon our friendship," I said.

"Indeed. You do this sort of thing often, do you not, speaking to people whose conversations you would never dream to seek in ordinary circumstance. Such as when you played billiards with me at Astley Close while you looked into the Westin affair."

I gave her a smile. "Touché."

"You did not like me, but you wanted information. I thought you a vacant-headed toady of Grenville's, and I sought to teach you a lesson, but I failed in that regard. You intrigued me mightily, you know."

"I am honored."

"Cease the Spanish coin, Captain. I will help you, because you are never interested in a thing unless it is worth the interest." Her eyes took on a mischievous sparkle. "But if I am to do you this favor, Captain, you must do me one in return."

"Of course," I said at once. "Tell me what it is, and I am your servant."

"I highly doubt that. I will ask you when I am finished interrogating Lady Clifford."

I had to wonder what she had in mind, but I was happy that she was willing to help. "I will be obliged to you," I said.

"Goodness, you must truly be fascinated by the

Clifford problem if you rashly promise that. But do not worry. I will discover what I can—discreetly—and report to you. Lady Clifford loves to talk about herself, in any case. I do not imagine I will have much difficulty."

"Could you contrive to speak to Mrs. Dale, as well? I very much would like to talk to her, but I've never met the woman."

"I will manage it." Lady Breckenridge spoke with firm self-confidence. "I believe she is an opium eater."

I stared. "Mrs. Dale?"

"Very likely in the form of laudanum. She has the look—red-rimmed eyes, rather pasty complexion, trembles a bit but strives to hide it. Such things happen."

Indeed, some people took laudanum for legitimate ailments, as I did when the pain in my leg proved too great, but then they could not leave off when they felt better. Poets apparently produced works of genius in this state. Grenville had an aversion to laudanum, even a fear.

"Tell me, Lacey," Lady Breckenridge said. She straightened up and sat neutrally, no artifice. "Why are you so interested in this theft? Aside from making certain your galumphing Runner does not arrest and hang the wrong person, that is. The solution is simple. Lady Clifford sold the necklace to pay her debts, she tried to push the blame on her rival, and her maid inadvertently was arrested instead. The problem is ended."

"Perhaps," I said. I rubbed my thumb over my engraved name on the walking stick. "But there seems to be more to it. And truth to tell, when I found Lady

Clifford in such misery, I wanted to help her. Doubly after I met her husband."

"Yes, Clifford is ghastly. You are quite the romantic, Captain Lacey, ever one to assist a lady in distress."

"Sometimes there is no one else to care," I said. "If that is romantic, then so be it."

Lady Breckenridge rose, came to me as I got to my feet, and put her hand over my much larger one. "It is one of the reasons I have decided to call you friend." She rose on her tiptoes and pressed a light kiss to my cheek. "Now, do go away. I must dress if I am to pay a sympathy call on Lady Clifford."

AS I LEFT LADY BRECKENRIDGE'S HOUSE AND walked down the street to find a hackney, I felt anew her kiss on my cheek. It reminded me of other kisses she'd given me, on the lips, as well as the few precious times her head had rested on my shoulder. My mood, soured by the encounter with James Denis and the dressing down Lord Clifford had given us, lightened considerably.

I had the hackney driver let me out at Southampton Street, and I ducked into the Rearing Pony for a restorative measure of good, bitter ale before walking home.

The city was darkening, clouds rolling in to spoil the sunshine and drench us in more rain. The last shoppers were purchasing supper in Covent Garden as I made my way through, and I paused to be entertained by a troupe of acrobats near one corner.

I continued the short way down Russel Street and turned in at Grimpen Lane, and made for the outside door next to the bake shop that led upstairs to my rooms. Mrs. Beltan, my landlady, who owned the shop, stood at her doorstep to watch me approach, looking impatient.

"There you are, Captain," she called. "I wasn't certain what to do. A gentleman has called on you, and I didn't want to let him up in your rooms without you here." She stepped close to me as I neared her and lowered her voice to a furtive whisper. "He is *French*."

CHAPTER 5

I looked past Mrs. Beltan into the shop and the gentleman there. The man was on the small side, with gray hair cropped close against a fine-boned face. He wore respectable clothing, nothing very costly. I did not know him, but he looked harmless.

"Sir," I nodded at him as I entered the shop. "We can talk in my rooms above and let this good lady retire."

The man bowed back to me. "Thank you, monsieur."

His accent was quite thick, as though he spoke English only when he could not avoid doing so. I stood back to let him pass and tipped my hat to the anxious-looking Mrs. Beltan.

"Do not worry," I murmured. "The war is over. I doubt we'll reenact Vitoria in my sitting room."

Mrs. Beltan gave me a displeased look, but she shrugged her plump shoulders and retreated. I took the unknown Frenchman upstairs and unlocked the door to my rooms.

Bartholomew had already stoked the fire, though the lad was nowhere in sight. The Frenchman moved to the fire and held his hands out to it. The coming rain had turned the evening cold.

"How can I help you, sir?" I asked.

He turned and regarded me with a cool gray stare. Though he was, as I'd observed, a small-boned man, he held himself with dignity, almost arrogance. "I have heard that you are a man to be trusted, Captain Lacey. A man of honor."

"I make that attempt, yes."

I closed the door behind me but didn't lock it then moved to the cupboard for brandy and two glasses. I had no worries about offering my brandy to a haughty Frenchman, because Grenville had given the stuff to me, so it was the best France could supply.

The man stood silently as I poured out and brought him a glass. He passed the goblet I handed him under his nose, then his expression changed to that of a man who'd unexpectedly come upon paradise.

He closed his eyes as he poured a little brandy into his mouth, then he pressed his lips together and rocked his head back in pure delight.

When he opened his eyes, I saw tears in them. "Thank you, sir. This is exquisite. I have not tasted such . . . in many years." He spoke heavily and slowly, pausing to make a low "hmm" noise in his throat.

"My friend Mr. Grenville has impeccable taste," I said. "You are an émigré?"

He had the bearing of wealth and breeding, but his

cheap clothes, his heavy accent, and the fact that he was in London at all told me he'd fled France long ago, when Madame Guillotine had been searching for victims.

"I am. I was. . . hmm . . . once the Comte de Mercier du Lac de la Fontaine. A long time ago now. Now the English call me Monsieur Fontaine."

An aristocrat, which explained the bearing. Likely the master of a vast estate, with hundreds of peasants toiling to keep him in silk stockings and the best brandy. All gone in the blink of an eye. I wagered that Fontaine's estate was now in the hands of a nouveau riche banker from Paris.

My wife lived somewhere in France, in a small village with her French officer lover. I doubted that this man knew her—I was willing to believe he'd fled France when the first danger had flared in Paris, before England and France went to war.

"What may I do for you, Monsieur le Comte?" I asked.

"My daughter, she is . . . hmm . . . married to an Englishman of some respectability. He is a member of White's club and quite proud of the fact." De la Fontaine gave me the ghost of a smile. I envisioned a pompous young Englishman pleased with himself that he'd landed the daughter of a French count.

"Do I know him?" I asked.

"It is possible you have met him, but he holds himself above all but the . . .hmm . . . top of society. He is acquainted with your friend, Mr. Grenville."

Which meant that Grenville at least tolerated the man. If Grenville had disapproved of this son-in-law, he would have found himself eventually pushed out of his precious White's.

"I can't speak for Grenville," I said. "If you wish me to ask him something on your behalf, I can't promise to. I suggest that you write to him yourself."

Monsieur de la Fontaine's smile vanished, and the cold aristocrat returned. In spite of his cheaply made suit, he had the bearing of a leader, one whose ancestors had held their corner of France in an iron grip.

"No, indeed, Captain," he said stiffly. "I have come to speak to *you*. About this affair of the stolen diamonds."

"Lady Clifford's necklace?" I asked in surprise.

"Not . . . hmm . . . Lady Clifford's, Captain. Mine. The diamonds that this English comtesse wishes you to find belong to me."

THINKING IT THROUGH, I DECIDED I SHOULD NOT BE very astonished. At the end of the last century, French émigrés had sold what they could in order to flee France, sometimes giving ship captains everything they had in return for being smuggled across the channel. The necklace had been made in Paris, the pawnbroker I'd spoken to had told me. Everything fit together.

"Captain, may we sit?" de la Fontaine asked.

I noticed his hands trembling. He might once have been a proud aristocrat, but now he was an elderly man, his bones aching with the rain.

"Of course." I gestured him to the wing chair, the most comfortable in the room and closest to the fire. I refilled his brandy while I dragged my desk chair over to his and sat.

Another sip of brandy restored the comte's stern but dignified stare. "Do you believe me?" he asked.

"I do," I said. "The necklace came from your family?"

The count tapped the arm of the chair with his brandy glass. He was angry, and holding the anger in. "The diamonds entered the de la Fontaine family during the time of Richelieu. They were . . . hmm . . . handed down through the generations. Cut, re-cut, set, and reset. They reached their present form in the middle of the last century, when my grandfather was the trusted confidant of the king's official mistress. She had them set into the necklace as a gift to him. My grandfather gave them to my father, who gave them to my mother on their marriage. When my mother passed, they came to me, and I determined to give them to my own daughter when she married. My only son was killed fighting Napoleon for the English, and my daughter is all that is left of the de la Fontaines."

He caught my sympathy and my amazed interest. A necklace created by the mistress of Louis XV would be worth far more than the several thousand pounds Lady Clifford had claimed the necklace cost. James Denis's interest also became clear. Denis would not concern himself with a simple lady's necklace, but he'd consider one with such a history well worth his notice.

"Why the devil does Earl Clifford have it, then?" I asked. "Did you sell him the necklace to pay your way out of France?"

The anger built in de la Fontaine's eyes. "I never

sold it, Captain. Everything else, yes. Hmm. Everything. To save my daughter, it was worth it. But I kept the necklace. It was her legacy. Then it was stolen from me. I had it before I crossed the Channel—when I arrived on this shore, it was gone."

"The ship's captain? Or crew?"

He shrugged. "In France, I had met an Englishman —Lord Clifford—who'd agreed, for a very large sum, to arrange passage for me and my daughter and son. My wife had succumbed to illness the year before, and my children were all I had left. I feared for their lives, and so we went. The voyage was fairly easy, and the captain seemed sympathetic. But when we disembarked, I discovered the meager belongings I'd managed to carry were all gone, and we had nothing but the clothes on our backs. When I reached London, I applied to Clifford for help, but was turned away at his front door. I was too proud to beg at his scullery for scraps, so I walked away. But the necklace was gone— I assumed stolen by the captain or one of his men. Lost forever. It . . . hmm . . . broke my heart. But at least I was alive and safe and so were my children."

"I am very sorry for your circumstance," I said.

I too, had lost much at the hands of others, and he had my sympathy. My estimation of Lord Clifford, not high in the first place, took a decided plunge.

Fontaine leaned forward. "And then, one evening last summer, my daughter and her husband took me with them to Vauxhall." He chuckled, still with the humming sound. "Taking the old man out to entertain him. As we supped in the pavilion, Captain, I saw the necklace. The jewels belonging to my family were hanging boldly around the neck of Countess Clifford, wife of the Englishman who'd helped me and my children fly from France."

"You are certain it was the same?" Even as I asked it, I knew he had been.

"Very certain. My wife handed the necklace back to me the day she died, telling me she wished she could have seen our daughter wearing it. I walked up to Lady Clifford and introduced myself. She pretended to remember me as an émigré her husband had helped, but I knew she had no idea who I was. She never once blushed that she wore my daughter's inheritance, as you say, under my nose."

"It is likely she did not know," I said. "I've met Lord Clifford."

"Then you know what sort of man he is. I'd not have taken his assistance at all had I not been desperate. That night, he knew that I knew, but he looked at me and . . . hmm . . . dared me to say a word."

"You did not go to a magistrate? Report the theft?"

"I am French, I am in exile. You have just finished a long war with France, and even the fact that my son lost his life fighting Napoleon for the English has not made me beloved here. What am I to tell a magistrate? I have only my word. Any paper about it, any proof I have that the necklace belongs to the de la Fontaines is long gone. Earl Clifford, he has money and influence. I have . . ." He opened his hand. "Nothing."

He was correct. De la Fontaine knew he could not prove the diamonds had belonged to him, and even I had to decide whether to believe him. He could be luring me into finding the necklace and giving it to him, whereupon he'd be several thousand pounds richer, and I'd be in the dock.

But I did not think he lied. De la Fontaine did not have the bearing and manner of a liar, and I could verify the story by browbeating Lord Clifford—a task I'd cheerfully perform.

"And what do you wish me to do?" I asked.

De la Fontaine finished his brandy, set down the glass, and rested his hands on his knees. "What I would wish is for you to find and return the necklace to me, and tell the earl that you have failed in your quest."

"And the moment your daughter wears the necklace to a soiree with your respectable English son-in-law? She or he will be accused of stealing it. Or at least of purchasing stolen goods."

He closed his eyes. "I know. I have no solution. I considered having the stones reset, but given its provenance . . ."

The fact that Madame de Pompadour had commissioned the necklace would be worth as much as the diamonds themselves. I appreciated his dilemma.

"Then I do not understand why you believe I can help," I said.

De la Fontaine opened his eyes. He had deep blue eyes, and now they looked old and tired. "I want someone to know the truth. I want you to find the diamonds and make certain they are safe. If they must reside with Lady Clifford forever, then so be it."

His resignation decided the question for me. Remembering Clifford snarling at Grenville that he ought to be ashamed to interest himself in the affair, and then watching this aged, exiled man slump in defeat, angered me not a little.

"You may leave things in my hands," I said. "I might be able to find you some justice."

De la Fontaine shook his head, his ghost of a smile returning. "Do not make promises, Captain. I have grown used to losing."

I rose, made my way to the brandy decanter, and poured him another glass. We'd finish all the brandy quickly at this rate, but Grenville would be happy to know it had been drunk by two men who appreciated it.

"Why do you not return to France?" I asked as the liquid trickled into his glass. "The king is restored, the emperor dead. There is peace now."

Fontaine saluted me with his goblet before he drank. "All I had in France is gone. My daughter is here, married to her fussy Englishman, and I have grandchildren who are growing rapidly. This has been my life for nearly thirty years. I have no reason to return."

I nodded, understanding. I was much like him—except for the fact of his ancestors ruling France and having diamonds set for them by Louis XV's beautiful mistress. My ancestors had been wealthy landholders, but their little estate in Norfolk was as nothing compared to the vast acreage this man must have commanded.

Now we both had nothing, reduced to wearing secondhand clothes and enjoying brandy gifted to us by a wealthy acquaintance. Out of place, wondering how this came to be, and not knowing what to do with ourselves.

We did finish the brandy. De la Fontaine seemed to want to linger, and I let him. He asked me how I came by my injury, and winced in sympathy when I described how I'd been beaten to a bloody pulp by a band of French soldiers then strung up by the ankles. One of the more sympathetic men had cut me down after a time, but when English and Prussian soldiers had attacked the French deserters' camp, killing them to the last man, they hadn't noticed me among the dead.

De la Fontaine shook his head at my story and told me how his son had been in the infantry, dying at Badajoz. I hadn't met the young man—I'd been cavalry in the Thirty-Fifth Light Dragoons, and we'd been fairly snobbish about the infantry.

"Bad fighting there," I said. "Brave lad."

"*Oui*. So I have heard."

We finished the decanter in silence. When de la Fontaine made to depart, I gave him a box of finely blended snuff—another gift from Grenville. I rarely took snuff, preferring a pipe the rare times I took tobacco, but de la Fontaine thanked me profusely.

I led him back down the stairs, and we took leave of each other. De la Fontaine shook my hand in the English way, lips twitching when he saw me bracing myself for a farewell in the French way.

Still smiling, he walked down Grimpen Lane, a bit unsteadily, through the rain. I leaned on the doorframe and watched him, wondering how the devil I was going to find the blasted necklace for him.

~

THREE DAYS PASSED. I TOLD GRENVILLE ABOUT DE
la Fontaine's visit and his assertion that the necklace
was his. Grenville professed to be amazed, and his
anger and disgust at Lord Clifford escalated to match
my own.

Grenville and I continued searching for the necklace, taking into account Lady Breckenridge's intelligence that a lady wishing to sell her jewels to pay her
creditors would find someone very discreet to make the
transaction for her. Her man of business, perhaps, if
she could hide such a dealing from her husband.

However, when Grenville and I visited Lady Clifford's man of business, we found a dry, very exact man
who seemed to march in step with Lord Clifford
regarding household affairs. Ladies were fools and
ought to do nothing without the approval of their
husbands. In his opinion, Lady Clifford had carelessly
lost the necklace and tried to pretend it stolen to shift
the blame from herself.

This left us no further forward.

I could see that Grenville was losing interest in the
problem. Lord Clifford's grumbles about Grenville
poking his nose into other gentlemen's business were
beginning to circulate through the *ton*. While Grenville
refused to bow to public opinion—any indication that
he cared about such a thing could spell his downfall—
he also did not believe there was much more to be
done. Though Grenville agreed that de la Fontaine's
story was creditable, he also suspected that the necklace would never see the light of day.

I saw that I would be soldiering on alone. I had not yet heard from Lady Breckenridge, but I did hear again from Denis, whose carriage pulled in behind me when I left Grenville's on a wet evening three days after de la Fontaine's visit.

The rain that had begun the afternoon I'd met de la Fontaine had continued with little abatement. The downpour was not as freezing as a winter rain, but still as drenching. When the carriage halted next to me and the door opened, I could not help but yearn for the warmth of its plush interior, in spite of the coldness of the man inside.

"De la Fontaine," Denis began as soon as I was sitting opposite him, the carriage moving on its way to Covent Garden. "One of the wealthiest men in France before the terror. Now living in a back bedroom in his proper English son-in-law's house, treated like a poor relation." Denis shook his head, but no emotion crossed his face. "Not a happy tale."

CHAPTER 6

I do not remember mentioning de la Fontaine to you," I said. Not that I was amazed that Denis knew all about de la Fontaine's visit to my rooms. He kept himself well informed.

"He is quite right about the necklace's provenance," Denis said, ignoring my statement. "A heavy blow to him that he lost it."

"Am I correct in guessing that you did not know that Lord Clifford had de la Fontaine's famous necklace?" Unusual for Denis, who hired people to roam Europe looking for such things for him, the rightful ownership of which was, to Denis, a trivial matter.

"I confess that I did not." Denis's brows drew together the slightest bit, a sign that the man behind the cold eyes was angry. "Hence why I wish to examine the piece myself. I knew the de la Fontaine necklace had disappeared many years ago, but not until Lady Clifford made a fuss about hers being stolen and involved Bow Street did it come to my attention that the two were one and the same. I had not thought Clifford resourceful enough to steal such a thing, but perhaps he seized an opportunity. Or perhaps the ship's captain stole it and sold it to Clifford, neither man appreciating what it was." Again the small frown. "Clifford owes me much money and has been reluctant to pay. He might have reported the necklace stolen to prevent himself from having to sell it to pay me, or in case I took it in lieu."

"Lord Clifford owes you money," I said. "I might have known."

"Many gentlemen owe me. Including you."

I let the remark pass. It was an old argument.

"If Clifford were to sell the necklace," I asked, "or his wife were to, how would they go about such a thing? Beyond common pawnbrokers and jewelers I mean. Who would they contact?"

Denis gave me a touch of a smile. "Me. I know of no other who could discreetly dispose of so obvious a piece."

"But if they did not realize what it was?"

"They might try the usual avenues, of course, but as soon as it came onto the market, jewelers in the know would put two and two together. Most likely the jewelers or pawnbrokers would offer the necklace to me, or at least ask for my help in shifting it."

"And you have not heard of it coming up for sale?"

"No. Not yet."

I twisted my walking stick under my hand. "If you do hear of it, will you tell me?"

"As I said, I want a look at it first."

"I am aware of that. But I've pledged myself to find it. Will you tell me?"

Denis regarded me in silence while I kept twisting the stick. There was a sword inside the cane, a fact he well knew.

When he spoke, Denis's voice held a careful note. "You have done me good turns in the past, Captain, and you are fair-minded. But I like to keep the balance clean, or at least bending slightly in my favor. If I do keep you in the know regarding this necklace, I will expect a like intelligence in return."

I hadn't the faintest idea what I could know that would interest him, but I was certain he'd come up with something devious. Denis liked things all his own way.

"It is a simple matter," I said. "I want to be informed if the necklace comes up for sale or when you lay your hands on it."

"Certainly. I will allow you to be in on the bidding."

"Bidding?" I clenched the walking stick, which stopped its twirl.

"If the necklace proves to be the de la Fontaine diamonds, I will assuredly wish to sell it," Denis said. "I am not in the business of assisting impoverished French émigrés or feckless English aristocrats. Clifford owes me money, and whatever price I can obtain for the necklace will more than suffice to pay his debt. He will not fight me for it."

"The necklace is de la Fontaine's," I said angrily.

"De la Fontaine's family stole the original diamonds themselves, you might be interested to learn, during some continental war long ago. And who knows from whence it was originally looted? Such famous pieces often have murky histories."

"You are splitting hairs. The necklace belongs to de la Fontaine, and I intend to give it back to him."

Another twitch of lips. "Of course you do. I will inform you if I come into possession of it, to that I will agree."

I sat still and looked at him, the impeccably dressed young man, kid-gloved hands folded on his walking stick.

I wondered, as I always did, how he'd come to be like this. Who was James Denis? What of his family? What sort of child had he been that he'd become a man who bought and sold precious objects, people, secrets? Had he loved and lost? Raised himself from nothing? Or been defeated and climbed out of the ashes?

If I asked, he'd never tell me, so I did not ask.

Denis looked at me as though guessing my thoughts. He knew by now exactly where I'd come from, who my people were, and what I'd done for the last forty years of my life. Denis was that thorough. I would have to be just as thorough about him.

One of his brows twitched upward. "Did you truly think I would tell you exactly where to find the necklace, Captain?" he asked. "It is worth far more than Lord Clifford understands. De la Fontaine understands. Perhaps it will ease your conscience if I tell you how many peasants de la Fontaine and his family worked to death in France during the height of their power. They lived quite well on the backs of many."

I knew that if de la Fontaine had come from landed wealth, then yes, he'd worked it out of others. But I couldn't help thinking of the broken man whose only joy these days was the chance sampling of Grenville's brandy and the occasional treat outing with his daughter and her stuffy husband.

"Have you become a republican?" I asked Denis.

He gave me a small shrug. "I must believe in every man being allowed to do what is best for himself, or I would be out of business."

He fell silent to look out the window at the rain, the conversation finished. We didn't speak until Covent Garden, where Denis had his coachman halt, and he bade me good night.

Now four people wanted the necklace: Lady Clifford, Lord Clifford, de la Fontaine, and Denis. Five people. Me.

I'd find the damn thing, and to hell with the lot of them. I would check de la Fontaine's story, and if he hadn't told me false, he would win the diamonds. I'd do something to placate Lord Clifford to keep him from turning his wrath on Lady Clifford. Clifford was the sort of man to blame his wife for his troubles. I cared nothing for what Denis thought of the matter. He'd find some other piece of art or jewelry on which to turn his attention soon enough.

When I entered my rooms in Grimpen Lane, Bartholomew was there, my fire roaring, my coffee hot. There were compensations for allowing him to practice valeting on me.

"Post's come," he said, pointing to a small pile of

letters on my writing table. "I say, Captain, Mr. Grenville is asking for my help tonight. I've got your dinner in. Can you manage on your own?"

"It will be a struggle," I said, sitting down at the writing table. Bartholomew had left a plate of beef in juice sitting perilously close to my post.

Bartholomew grinned. "Aye, sir. I'll be back before morning."

"Stay at Grenville's and return tomorrow. No need for you to be rushing across town in the middle of the night in the rain. I can manage to hobble downstairs for a bit of bread on my own for breakfast."

"Are you certain, sir?" Bartholomew liked to believe I'd be hopelessly lost without him. "I can tell Mr. Grenville you can't spare me if you like."

"Mr. Grenville pays your wages, not me. What entertainment is he having tonight? I'm not expected, am I?"

"No, sir. It's his circle of art fanciers. They have supper and talk about Constable and Dah-veed and that French chap with the name like the sound of your throat closing up."

"Ingre?" I asked.

"That's the sausage. Sorry, sir, Mr. Grenville didn't tell me to tell you to come."

"Thank God for that. I'm hardly in the mood to talk about the intricacies of David and his pupils. David was a radical revolutionary, did you know that? Probably ran Comte de la Fontaine out of his home personally, thereby allowing de la Fontaine to be preyed upon by an Englishman looking to line his coffers. Possibly best I do not bring this up at Grenville's supper with his art critics."

"No, sir." Bartholomew gave me a dubious glance. He never knew what to do with me when I started waxing philosophical.

"Never mind. Go on, then."

Bartholomew poured me more coffee then made ready to depart with a look of relief.

I was glad to see him go, because I'd recognized the handwriting on the top letter of the pile as that of Lady Breckenridge, and I wanted to read her missive in private. I shoveled in beef and bread while Bartholomew scrambled upstairs to gather a few things to take home with him.

As soon as Bartholomew had trundled down the stairs and out — slamming the door hard behind him — I wiped my hands, broke the seal on the letter, and opened it.

My dear Lacey, Lady Breckenridge wrote. *I think that I shall never forgive you for persuading me to undertake this decidedly dreadful task. I must invent many more favors for you to do in return.*

I smiled, but with a touch of uneasiness, and read on.

I have been seeing much of Lady Clifford of late, and I cannot express what a relief it is to return to my quiet home in the evenings. Barnstable brings me thick coffee, which he liberally laces with brandy, bless him. Though I believe an entire decanter of the stuff would not be enough to rid myself of the taste of the Clifford household. Heaven help you, Lacey.

But I will cease complaining and come to the heart of the matter. It was easy enough to worm myself into Lady Clifford's household. I approached Lady Clifford on the pretext of asking her to assist me with one of my musicales — there is a soprano who sings like an angel — I believe you will agree when you hear her.

Who knows why Lady Clifford so readily believed I sought her help. Her taste in music is appalling — or, I should say, nonexistent. But I soldiered on, and she professed delight.

The poor woman has not much more to do in her life but play cards and gossip. Even her companion, Mrs. Dale, does all the embroidery for her, while Lady Clifford sits and pretends to conduct interesting conversation. She does knit on occasion, for the poor, though so badly that I suspect the poor simply unravel the yarn and use it for some more practical purpose.

These drawbacks are not entirely her fault. Her husband, I have now observed firsthand, tells Lady Clifford outright that anything she endeavors is foolish, and so she gives up before she begins. Lord Clifford tried to include me in one of these rants but, as you can imagine, he had no success in that regard.

Lady Clifford is much too easily cowed by him. Bullies are encouraged by meekness, as I have come to know.

Mrs. Dale, the companion, is not as easily cowed, but her strength lies in her silences. She is able to remain perfectly still, eyes on her sewing, no matter what storms rage on around her. She is not quiet like a serene pool — more like a stubborn rock that refuses to be worn down. Because of this, she hasn't much to say for herself, although I note that, when we ladies are alone, some rather sarcastic humor comes out of her mouth. Not often, but it is there.

Mrs. Dale does indeed take laudanum, as I suspected. Her excuse is headache, which, she says, is why she likes to sit so quietly, but that is all fabrication. When anything unnerving happens in that household, it's a quick nip from the laudanum bottle. And believe me Lacey, unnerving things occur all the time.

For instance, Mrs. Dale mislaid Lady Clifford's knitting basket (on purpose, I suspect). Instead of simply telling a servant to find the blasted thing, Lady Clifford went into hysterics. She screeched at Mrs. Dale about her every fault, until Lord Clifford, who was home, had to come to see what was the matter.

I stepped to the next room, pretending the need to refresh myself—and indeed, I was developing a headache as fierce as Mrs. Dale's supposed ones. I heard Lord Clifford quite clearly tell his wife that the loss of the knitting basket was her own fault, that she could not keep account of any damned thing, and there was a reason he'd begun to favor Mrs. Dale over her.

I am not certain he'd have said such a thing had he known I was listening, but then again, Lord Clifford hasn't the best of manners. But really, what a thing to tell your wife! Lady Clifford cried all the more, Mrs. Dale joined her when Lord Clifford stormed out, and I returned to two weeping women.

But interestingly, I found them trying to console each other. Dear, dear Annabelle wasn't to blame, said Lady Clifford, and Mrs. Dale cried that dear, dear Marguerite was brave to suffer so much.

They continued weeping and embracing even after I sat down and pointedly started going through the guest list for the musicale. I gather that the two were the dearest of friends before Lord Clifford decided he wanted both his meat and his sauce in his own house. Saves him the bother of going out for it, I suppose. The two ladies are putting up with it as best they can.

The truce did not last long, however. Before another hour was out, Mrs. Dale was once more a hard-hearted, ungrateful bitch, and Lady Clifford a slow-witted fool.

I took Mrs. Dale aside and asked her why she stuck it here. I do not for one moment believe that she has fallen in love with Lord Clifford. From all evidence, she rather despises him.

Mrs. Dale blinked red-lined eyes at me and bleated that she stayed because she had nowhere else to go. This I can well credit. Her husband hadn't a penny left to his name when he died, and Mrs. Dale immediately went to live with her girlhood friend, Lady Clifford. She's been in the house ever since. Mrs. Dale did not say this, but I also had the feeling that she does not want to leave Lady Clifford to face Lord Clifford on her own.

Both ladies are well under Lord Clifford's thumb, and I strongly suspect that his interest in Mrs. Dale is more a game of power over his wife than any sort of sentimental feeling.

This was confirmed by my maid who spent the time in the kitchens while I was there (and by the bye, she is not very forgiving of you, either). Lord Clifford apparently satisfies some of his baser needs with maids below stairs, including the very maid arrested for stealing the necklace.

Of the necklace itself, I haven't a dratted clue. I have run very tame in Lady Clifford's house but have been unable to find a trace of it. I began with the most obvious place, Lady Clifford's own bedchamber and dressing room. The woman has many baubles—Lord Clifford does not stint on hanging finery on her. He must be of the ilk that believes a jewel-encrusted wife reflects well on him. However, the necklace in question was nowhere in Lady Clifford's chambers that I could see.

Next was Mrs. Dale's meager chamber, but again, I had no luck. What I discovered there was that Mrs. Dale wears Lady Clifford's castoff gowns, modified to fit her rather narrower figure. Her jewelry is quite modest. Again, I suspect, gifts from her dear Lady Clifford before their falling out.

Lord Clifford might favor Mrs. Dale in his bed these days, but he certainly hasn't rewarded her with anything costly. Or, if he has, she neither displays these gifts nor keeps them in her bedchamber. I assure you, I was quite thorough.

Other rooms revealed nothing. I could not do much searching in the main sitting room, because Lady Clifford and Mrs. Dale were sitting in it. Constantly. I took a quick look at the dining room, but I had little time, and it's likely anything hidden there would be found by a servant.

Not that the staff of Lady Clifford's house is anything like efficient. I would sack the lot of them, and I told the housekeeper so. The housekeeper is an exhausted stick, not pretty enough for Lord Clifford, I gather, and he does run rather hard on her when he bothers to notice her at all. Were it my lot in life to be a housekeeper, I'd certainly try to find a better place.

Nonetheless, the servants at least attempt to keep the large house clean, and anything hidden in the public rooms would come to light eventually. That leaves the kitchens, the chambers of the servants themselves, and Lord Clifford's private study and bedchamber.

A servant might hide the necklace for her employer out of loyalty, but I do not think so in this case. I have not seen here the sort of affection some servants have for their employers. Barnstable looks after me as though he still regards me as the naïve young wretch who first married Breckenridge, ages ago it seems now. The staff in the Clifford household simply do their jobs, and from what my maid tells me, the family is not much respected below stairs.

As I say, that leaves Lord Clifford's private study and bedchamber. If I can contrive to enter them, I will, but apparently, there is but one reason a lady enters Lord Clifford's bedchamber, and forgive me, Lacey, but there is a limit to my interest in this little problem. Lord Clifford's chamber might have to go unsearched.

I am afraid this letter will not help you much. In conclusion, if the stolen necklace is still in the house, it is well hidden. And if it secretly has been sold, I cannot tell either, because no one here ever discusses the necklace at all. A forbidden topic, I gather.

The atmosphere is strained and full of anger, and Lady Clifford, Mrs. Dale, and Lord Clifford make a strange threesome. There is no love lost between them, and much misery exists.

Now, then, Lacey, in return for my prying, I will ask one of my favors right away—and that is for you to attend said musicale tonight. I have observed that you dislike crowded gatherings, but you must put a brave face on it and come. If nothing else, your presence will give me a chance to speak more to you about this problem.

Wear your grand uniform and stand about looking imposing, as you do, so that my guests will have something to talk about. They grow bored and need a good whisper about the captain friend of Grenville's who turns up at Lady Breckenridge's gatherings now and again.

Besides, in truth, you will quite enjoy the soprano. Unlike Lady Clifford, I do have fine musical taste, and I shall have Barnstable look out for you.

Ever yours in friendship,
Donata Breckenridge

CHAPTER 7

*B*artholomew would not return tonight, so I had to dress myself for the musicale. Bartholomew was convinced I could no longer do this on my own, but he kept my clothes so clean that they always looked fine, no matter how clumsy I might be at buttoning my own coat.

I peered into the small square mirror in my bedroom as I brushed my thick hair and fastened the braid across my chest. The regimentals of the Thirty-Fifth Light consisted of a dark blue coat with silver braid and dark cavalry breeches with knee-high boots. I wore the regimentals for social occasions, this being the finest suit I owned.

Imposing, Lady Breckenridge had written. I glanced into the aging glass again. She either flattered me or poked fun at me.

I took a hackney across London to South Audley Street and entered Lady Breckenridge's house with a few moments to spare.

Lady Breckenridge prided herself on her musicales and soirees, styling herself as one of the tastemakers of London. Therefore, her sitting room was filled to overflowing, and I sidled through the crowd as politely as I could.

Sir Gideon Derwent was there, his kind face breaking into a smile when he saw me. Next to him was his son Leland, a slimmer, younger version of the father, and a pace behind them, Leland's great friend, Gareth Travers. The Derwents were a family of innocents who invited me to dine with them at their house in Grosvenor Square once a fortnight. There, they'd beg me to entertain them with stories of my army life. Travers had a bit more cynicism, but he seemed to enjoy the unworldly companionship of the Derwents as much as I did.

We took seats for the performance. Lady Breckenridge, dressed in a russet gown that bared her shoulders, introduced the lady as Mrs. Eisenhauf, a young Austrian who was just beginning her career. A pianist played a few strains on her instrument, and the soprano launched into her aria.

I found myself floating on a cushion of music, sound that filled my entire body. The woman's voice soared, loud and full, then dropped to the tiniest whisper, never losing its strength and quality.

Those around me were enchanted as well, but after a time, I stopped noticing anyone else. I heard only the music, observed only the curve of Lady Breckenridge's cheek, her face soft with enjoyment. Lady Breckenridge might once have been the naïve young wretch she described, but she'd left that girl far behind.

For a moment, I forgot about necklaces, weeping ladies, de la Fontaine's unhappiness, and the cold rain outside. There was only this bliss of warmth and music, and Lady Breckenridge's smile.

The aria ended, not in a crescendo, but in a few low notes of pure sweetness. As soon as the lady closed her mouth, the room erupted in applause and shouts of *Brava! Brava!*

They surged forward to meet her, swamping Lady Breckenridge, who stood next to her protégé. I wondered why Lady Breckenridge had brought me to this crush if she wished to speak to me privately as her letter had stated. I'd never get near her.

I spied Lady Clifford, dressed in a blue velvet gown too tight for her figure, her high feathered headdress bobbing as she moved among her acquaintance. Hearing snatches of her conversation, I learned that she took much of the credit for arranging the gathering and persuading the soprano to sing.

Lady Clifford spied me watching her. She made her way to me, clamped her hand around my arm, and drew me into a corner.

"Have you found the thief, Captain?" she asked, a bit too loudly for my taste.

"I am afraid I've turned up nothing, yet," I had to say.

"I wanted to tell you, I believe my husband was right that I made a mistake asking for your help." She smiled at me, but the smile was strained. "You have no more need to bestir yourself. Waters came home, and so that is all right. The real thief will be found by the Runners, eventually. Nothing more for you to do."

I hid my surprise at her request, but perhaps Lord Clifford had bullied her into dismissing me. "You at first believed Mrs. Dale had taken the necklace," I said. "You told me so."

Lady Clifford flushed a blotchy red. "As to that—I again made a mistake. Annabelle has many faults, but she would not be so foolish as to steal something so valuable as the necklace. I did not realize . . ."

She trailed off, not telling me what she hadn't realized.

"Did your husband tell you that I found your other necklace, Lady Clifford?" I asked.

"Other necklace? What other necklace?"

"The one you took to a pawnbroker near Hanover Square. Your husband identified it as a yours. Said it was a necklace you'd owned before your marriage."

Her flush deepened but I saw relief in her eyes. "Captain, really, you should not have interfered there. It was mine to sell as I pleased."

"You sent Waters to sell it for you, did you not? The proprietor described her."

"Yes, well I could not go myself, could I? Not to a pawnbroker's." She nodded so vigorously that her feathers bent and swayed as though she stood in a heavy wind. "I see what you are thinking, Captain. That I sold the larger diamond necklace as well, for my own reasons. Well, I did not. I certainly did not."

"I believe you," I said.

Her agitation dissolved into surprise. "Do you?"

"I do. Would you like me to continue to find the answer? And the necklace?"

"No," she said quickly. "I think it doesn't matter

anymore." She paused then shook her head, feathers dancing. "No, it does not. But I thank you, Captain. Thank you for believing me."

She clutched my arm again, fingers crushing, then at last released me and flowed back into the crowd.

I still could come nowhere near Lady Breckenridge, so I enjoyed myself sipping brandy and speaking to the Derwents and Gareth Travers. I asked Sir Gideon his opinion of Lord Clifford, and he gave me a surprising answer.

"Not a good-humored man, certainly. And his household is not a happy one, from what I hear. No, his benevolence lies elsewhere. He has given much money to help the London poor and is a staunch supporter of many of my reform efforts. He's made speeches in the House of Lords on my behalf."

I contrasted this picture to the snarling, unpleasant man I'd met, and Sir Gideon chuckled.

"You are amazed, Captain. Yes, it comes as a bit of a shock to those who have made his acquaintance. I offer no excuse for his demeanor. Some men are born surly, I suppose. But he was able to convince the magistrates to release his wife's maid. He speaks loudly to the right people about the appalling conditions of prisons and of corruption among magistrates. He was able to bring her home and have the charges dismissed."

"To think, I imagined this would be a simple matter," I said.

"Nothing is simple where Lord Clifford is concerned. He is a cipher, Captain, even to me."

I thanked Sir Gideon for his opinion, and we turned the conversation to other matters.

Guests seemed determined to stay until breakfast, but once the soprano said her farewells and departed, they began to migrate toward the doors. Lady Breckenridge edged me away from the lingerers, until we ended up relatively alone at the fireplace.

She put her hands to her cheeks. "My face hurts from all this bloody smiling. The things I suffer for my artists."

"But you enjoyed the performance," I said. "The pleasure I saw in you was real."

A hint of the earlier smile returned. "Yes," she said. "But cease the compliments and listen, before someone decides to drag me off into an inane conversation. I have something to tell you that was not in my letter. Which, I trust, you read carefully."

"Every word," I said. "It was quite intriguing."

"I am certain it was. However, when my maid was dressing me this evening, she imparted intelligence from Lady Clifford's kitchens. Waters, the maid, was enjoying telling her harrowing tale of Bow Street gaol and being up before the magistrate. Reprieved at the last moment by testimony from Lord Clifford."

"Sir Gideon has been telling me that Lord Clifford is a bit of a reformer who worries the magistrates."

"Gracious, there is more to the story than that. According to those below stairs, Lord Clifford was persuaded to intervene on the behalf of young Waters by Annabelle Dale. Begged him tearfully, said an upstairs maid, who overheard the conversation. Apparently, Mrs.

Dale asked Lord Clifford to help for 'poor, dear Marguerite's sake. We must all do what we can to spare Marguerite.' Extremely interesting, do you not think?"

Exceedingly. *Spare Marguerite.* Spare her from what?

"Life in the Clifford household must certainly be interesting," I said with feeling.

"I agree." Lady Breckenridge glanced across the room at Lady Clifford, and her mouth tightened with impatience. "I believe I will be more careful of the favors I do you in future."

"Investigating crime is not always a pleasant thing."

"I never thought it was. Certainly nothing for a gentleman or a lady who knows better. But that is why you interest me, Lacey. You never do what you ought."

"Nor do you."

The look she gave me was measuring. "But I am an aristocrat and have the excuse of being removed from my fellow beings. You must strive to be utterly respectable, and yet, you do not always bother. I believe that is why I like you."

"I am obliged to you for that liking."

She regarded me for one more moment, her expression unreadable. "I can never decide, Lacey, whether you are complimenting me or mocking me, but it is no matter. I see that Lady Clifford has cornered an admiral. I am afraid I must rescue him. Good night, Captain."

I bowed. "My lady."

She sashayed away, throwing that sincere smile over her shoulder, and I stood for a moment, enjoying watching her go.

As I left the Breckenridge house, settling my hat against the rain, I wondered. Had Mrs. Dale actually taken the bloody necklace as Lady Clifford had first suspected? Just as she'd hidden Lady Clifford's knitting basket and caused a scene? Perhaps guilt had made her beg Lord Clifford to bring home the maid. Or perhaps Mrs. Dale had shown benevolence toward the maid to land herself in Lady Clifford's good graces again.

Whatever the answer was, I was growing thoroughly tired of this problem. It was late, the cold rain made my injured leg throb, and after the beauty of the soprano's voice and Lady Breckenridge's smiles, all else seemed drab, dull, and not worth bothering about.

I would lie in bed all the next day, have Bartholomew fetch me coffee, read the newspapers, and tell my blasted curiosity to go away. I was cold and sore, and I deserved a rest. Earl Clifford and his odd household could worry someone else.

I became so enamored of this idea that I thought of little else as the hackney bumped me back to Covent Garden. Therefore, my dismay was great when I walked into my bedchamber and found a woman lying fast asleep between my sheets.

CHAPTER 8

I woke the woman without hesitation. "Marianne, what the devil are you doing?"

Marianne Simmons, actress from a Drury Lane company, once my upstairs neighbor, and now, in theory at least, Grenville's mistress, sat up and blinked china-blue eyes at me.

"Blast you, Lacey. Your voice is loud, and my head aches something awful. You weren't using your bed, so I saw no harm in borrowing it."

"I remember locking my door before I went out," I said.

"I stole your key months ago and had my own cut."

She could easily have done. I'd grown used to having Bartholomew here to let me in, plus I'd spent most of the last month out of London. Marianne could have stolen the key from my drawer at any time, me none the wiser.

"I am too tired to argue with you," I said. "Make use of the bed if you must, and I'll adjourn to

Bartholomew's attic. Tomorrow you can tell me why you aren't sleeping in the house Grenville keeps so nicely for you."

"*That* is none of your affair. And good heavens, the attics must be freezing. This is a large bed, and there's a good fire. Plenty of room for both of us."

I was exhausted and aching, that was true. "I imagine myself explaining to Grenville why I was in a bed with you. He'll call me out for it, and then I'll have to let him shoot me, because I have no desire to kill him. My death will be on your head."

"Do not be ridiculous, Lacey. First, *he* is far more interested in supping with his art friends tonight than in calling on me. Second, you look all in. I'm certain a climb to the top of the house to a freezing room will kill you. When I was in a traveling company, we slept seven or eight to a bed such as this, too tired to do anything but snore." She scooted to the far right of the bed and patted the mattress beside her. "I promise not to touch you."

I believed her. Marianne, as far as I could tell, had very little interest in men apart from how much money they could give her. The exception was Grenville. She'd professed genuine confusion and not a little dismay that he'd not yet asked of her what most gentlemen asked of her.

I knew Marianne had no amorous designs on me—she regarded me as a person from whom she could borrow candles, coal, food, drink, snuff, and now, my bed. I use the word "borrow," but in truth Marianne never repaid what she took, whether in cash or in kind. I'd not stopped her, knowing that without what she took from me, she'd have gone hungry and cold many a night.

She was right that it was a long way to the top of the house, and Bartholomew relied only on the heat from the chimney. Fine for a robust youth, bad for a man twice his age whose stiff limb was hurting him very much tonight.

I smothered a sigh, went out to the front room, and stripped down to my shirt and drawers, and returned. I did not don the nightshirt that Bartholomew had left on the bed to warm, because Marianne had helped herself to that too.

The bedchamber was dark enough for modesty, and I slipped under the covers without having to blush. I admitted that the bed was nice and warm from Marianne's body, and true to her word, she kept herself on the far edge.

I lay back, tiredness and hurt overriding my common sense. "Be gone before Bartholomew returns in the morning," I said. "I might not be able to awaken you in time."

"Not to worry, Lacey. I am adept at covertly leaving a gentleman's bed."

"And never say such a thing to Grenville."

"Thank you, but I know how to manage *him*."

"Is being here part of your efforts to manage him?" I asked, closing my eyes.

"No, this is my effort at seeking a bit of quiet. You are the only person on this earth who does not plague me to tears."

"I am pleased to hear it."

I searched for the oblivion of slumber, but though I

had nearly nodded off in the hackney, my mind, treacherously, was now wide awake. My body wanted to sink into the dubious comfort of my mattress, but my thoughts could not rest, and I fidgeted.

The bed shifted, and I guessed without looking that Marianne had propped herself on one elbow. "Perhaps you should talk about it," she said. "Let loose what is in your head so that you can sleep."

So she might say to one of her paramours. I knew gentlemen who professed that what they most enjoyed about their mistresses was that the ladies actually listened to their troubles.

At this moment, talking was exactly what I needed. I found myself telling her everything, from the moment I'd met Lady Clifford in Grenville's private sitting room to my evening at Lady Breckenridge's musicale. I did not know how much of this Marianne already knew, but she listened with interest to my tale.

When I finished, I did indeed feel better. Quieter in mind, ready to let it all go for now and seek sleep.

"Lady Clifford and Mrs. Dale," Marianne said thoughtfully. "At each other's throats one minute, oozing affection for each other the next, then back to baleful glares? Do I have the right of it?"

"So Lady Breckenridge tells me. And now Lady Clifford has entirely changed her mind about accusing her rival and wanting me to investigate the matter. Damn the woman."

"Her rival," Marianne repeated. She went silent as she settled down and arranged the covers over her. "I've been an actress for a while, you know. I've worked in several companies, both meager and great.

When you are thrown side by side with men and women for long stretches at a time, where modesty and politeness go hang, you learn much about people."

"Seven or eight in a bed helps with that, presumably."

"Exactly. Men *and* women stuffed together. No privacy at all—for anything. Privacy is for the wealthy. What you describe of Lady Clifford and Mrs. Dale I've observed before, several times. Lowly actresses or highborn ladies, there really is not much difference, despite what people say."

"A love triangle is a triangle, no matter where it is placed, you mean?" I agreed with her. In the army, I had been thrown into close contact with men and women of all walks of life. Though rigorous care might be taken to separate the ranks, we all bathed, ate, loved, and died together.

"I mean that you are viewing the love triangle, if there is one, the wrong way around," Marianne said. "Not Lord and Lady Clifford broken apart by Mrs. Dale. I mean Lady Clifford and Mrs. Dale, broken apart by the maid, Waters."

My eyes opened. "Lady Clifford and Mrs. Dale?"

Marianne laughed. "Gentlemen are so shocked when they learn that women do not prefer them. It grates on their pride, I believe. But it happens more often than you like to think, and can you blame them? Men like Lord Clifford can be quite awful."

I lay still, thinking of the tangle in light of Marianne's speculations. "Lady Breckenridge never put forth this idea."

"Because Lady Breckenridge has no use for other

women, and so she does not watch them particularly closely. As horrible as her own husband was, she would never turn to ladies for consolation. And so, she might not recognize the need in others."

I turned my head to look at Marianne, unashamedly stretched out beside me, her head on my pillow. "And you?"

She shrugged. "I too, have little use for women, but I've been thrown among them far more than has your Lady Breckenridge. Lady Clifford and Mrs. Dale sound like lovers who had a falling out over something. Or someone. This Waters, is she pretty? And I imagine that Mrs. Dale has no choice but to comply when Lord Clifford makes advances to her. He could turn her out of his house, after all, if she resists."

And Mrs. Dale had professed to have nowhere else to go.

I let out a breath. "Good God."

"Think of it that way, and I'm certain it will help. Good night."

So saying, Marianne turned over, dragged the quilts over her, and fell fast asleep. Or at least, she pretended to.

Marianne had given me much to think about. Most people would believe, as I had, that Mrs. Dale and Lady Clifford were enraged at each other because of Lord Clifford's amorousness. Two women fighting to possess the same man.

But thinking on what Lady Breckenridge had told me, both women thoroughly disliked the bullying Lord Clifford. A romance between the ladies, on the other hand, especially if they'd quarreled over Lady Clifford's affection for her maid Waters, might explain Lady Clifford's spiteful accusation that Mrs. Dale had taken the necklace. It would explain her about-face on the matter as well.

Perhaps it hadn't been brought home to Lady Clifford what could happen to Mrs. Dale—Newgate, ignominy, hanging—until the maid, Waters, had returned to describe her harrowing ordeal.

It also threw into new light Lady Breckenridge's observation of the two women crying and hugging over the missing knitting basket. They'd been comforting each other after Lord Clifford's harangue—lovers who cared more about each other than for the brutal man who bullied them both.

Mrs. Dale had begged Lord Clifford to help bring Waters home. Because she felt sorry for her "dear Marguerite" and wanted to spare her more pain? Or to try to restore peace between herself and Lady Clifford? Both, possibly.

"Hell, Marianne," I said.

Marianne only snored.

TRUE TO HER WORD, MARIANNE WAS GONE BEFORE I woke. The window showed sunshine, the rain finished for now, the bed beside me empty. I heard Bartholomew in my front room, and a moment later, he strode into my bedchamber with his usual energy, coffee balanced on a tray.

"Did you not see your nightshirt?" he asked when he saw me in my underclothes. The garment lay across the bed again as though it had never been worn.

"I didn't bother to make a light," I said, extemporizing. "I was exhausted."

I felt a bit better this morning, although by the light outside the window, the day was already moving on to afternoon. Talking things over with Marianne, followed by a good night's sleep, had restored my vigor.

Bartholomew left the coffee and lifted the nightshirt. As I sat up and reached for the coffee, Bartholomew frowned at the nightshirt, then he delicately sniffed its collar. He raised his brows at me.

I took a nonchalant sip of coffee, telling myself he would not recognize Marianne's perfume. Bartholomew had started working for me before Grenville had taken up with Marianne, and the lad did not accompany Grenville on his visits to her in Clarges Street. Grenville had a different staff for that house, in any case.

"Not a word," I said.

Bartholomew drew himself up. "A gentleman's gentleman is discreet, sir."

"I know you are, Bartholomew. A bath, I think."

"Sir." Bartholomew went away, carrying the nightshirt over his arm.

As I bathed and let Bartholomew shave me, I again considered Marianne's revelation about Lady Clifford and Mrs. Dale.

I'd met two hermaphrodites, as people had called them, in the village where I'd grown up. They'd been elderly ladies, styling themselves as a lady and her companion. Everyone knew, but of course did not mention in public, that they were lovers, or at least had been.

I didn't remember much about them except that one was kind to me, and I couldn't remember to this day which had been the lady and which had been the companion. They'd passed away within months of each other when I'd been about nine years old. No one had bothered them, but then, they'd been two spinster ladies who'd lived quietly, well past the age of anyone's interest.

Lady Clifford, on the other hand, was a married lady prominent in society. And Mrs. Dale was a poor widow, dependent on others for her bed and board. Dangerous for any gossip about her to circulate. They would have to be secretive.

Last night I had thought about letting the investigation go, leaving the Clifford family to sort out their own troubles. But then, there was de la Fontaine. His tale had tugged at me. I knew that I sympathized with him because I felt he was like me—a long way from his old life, unsure of his place in the world, dependent on others when he did not want to be.

The necklace belonged to de la Fontaine. He should have it back.

To find it, I needed to speak to Lady Clifford again. After breakfasting, I penned a letter to Lady Breckenridge asking her to fix an appointment for me with Lady Clifford. I could imagine Lady Breckenridge's exasperation when she received the note, and I would be in her debt again, but I also knew that she'd arrange the meeting.

I decided to leave it at that and make my way to Hyde Park and the stables for a little exercise. At one time, I'd given riding lessons to a lad I'd met while investigating the Hanover Square problem. The lad's father stabled his beasts in Hyde Park and generously allowed me to ride one of his geldings whenever I liked, even now that the boy had returned to school. His father had told me he recognized a man who could handle horses right enough.

It was nearly two when I rode out, I having slept longer than usual. The fashionable hour wouldn't begin until five, but plenty of riders and drivers already moved about the park, enjoying the respite from the rain.

I walked and trotted the well-trained gelding, letting him canter a bit down an empty stretch of the Row. I turned down a lesser path to keep riding and spied Grenville astride his bay ahead of me, his tall hat shining in the sunshine.

I nudged my horse into a faster trot to catch up, but as I neared Grenville, another man on horseback swung out of an intersecting path. I recognized Lord Clifford, who began bellowing as he rode at Grenville.

"What do you mean by it, Grenville? Hounding a man's womenfolk until they're ill with it? My wife's life hung by a hair's breadth, all because of you and your interfering captain."

As I spurred my horse forward, Lord Clifford leaned down and tried to drag Grenville from the saddle.

CHAPTER 9

*M*y horse leapt forward in a burst of speed. Grenville's mount was already dancing sideways, Lord Clifford's doing the same. My long cavalry experience let me steer my gelding between them and wedge the two horses apart.

"What the devil?" Grenville said, out of temper. "Have a care, Clifford."

Lord Clifford was red-faced, spittle flecking his mouth. "What will you do, Grenville, have me thrown out of the Jockey Club? Doesn't matter. I refuse to be a member when fellows like you hold sway. You nearly killed my wife."

Clifford tried to ride around me and at Grenville again, but I remained firmly between Grenville's horse and Clifford's. I rode better than either of them, and Clifford would not get through me.

"Explain yourself," I said to him. "What happened?"

"My wife swallowed a large dose of laudanum last

night, that is what happened. Only the care of her ladies brought her back to life. She cited some nonsense about guilt and misery, and how she never ought to have spoken to either of you. You gentlemen have turned my house into Bedlam, and I will not have it."

"Is Lady Clifford well?" I asked quickly.

"She will recover. Likely she only took it for the attention, but this was your doing, Grenville. Stay the hell out of my private affairs."

With that, he turned his horse and spurred it cruelly. The horse leapt away, ears back, gravel flying from his hooves.

Grenville was breathing hard. "Damn the man. He is an ogre. He doesn't care that Lady Clifford might have died, only that her troubles have disrupted him." He removed a handkerchief from his black coat, brushed away the dust Clifford's horse had kicked up, and carefully folded the handkerchief again. "I will have to do something about him, I think."

"He is not wrong," I said. "Our interference, especially mine, did lead to her distress of mind, but something does not quite ring true. I spoke to Lady Clifford last evening. She told me she'd changed her mind about Mrs. Dale being the culprit, and that she no longer wanted me to pursue the matter. She was agitated about it, but hardly in a state to go home and take too much laudanum."

"Unless she did not administer it herself," Grenville said. "You did say that Lady Breckenridge believed Mrs. Dale drinks laudanum for pleasure. She'd have a bottle close at hand."

"Possibly, but why she'd want to kill Lady Clifford is unclear to me." I told Grenville the theory about Lady Clifford and Mrs. Dale being lovers, or at least former lovers, without implying that the idea had come from anywhere but my own head. Any mention of Marianne would likely turn this conversation in an uncomfortable direction.

"You might be right," Grenville said. "It's a very insular household, and something like that would be kept quiet. But does it have any bearing on the lost necklace?"

"I have no idea," I said. "I hoped to speak to Lady Clifford today, but . . ." I broke off. "I will try to find out."

"I, for one, will be pleased to be quit of Clifford and his family. They are devilish melodramatic."

While Grenville, I realized, disliked personal drama of any kind. No wonder Marianne drove him distracted.

"My boyhood home could be as melodramatic," I said. "Histrionics seemed to be the sought-after state, in my father, the housekeeper, the staff—anyone he controlled. My father was a bit like Lord Clifford, in fact."

Grenville straightened his hat, his face still red, but he regained his composure as I watched. "Well, I am pleased you turned out as well as you did, my dear fellow. My boyhood home was devoid of emotion at all. We were calm and careful from sunrise to sunset, sunset to sunrise. My father tolerated no dramatics of any kind. I'm not certain which is more devilish uncomfortable—too many emotions or none at all."

"Perhaps that is why you and I rub along well," I said. "I find your coolness restful, you find my volatility interesting."

Grenville raised his brows. "I do hope our friendship has progressed beyond that. Shall we ride on, Lacey? It is a fine afternoon, the park is not yet crowded, and I dislike to waste the opportunity simply because Clifford put me off."

He turned his horse and guided it onward, and I followed.

I admired Grenville's ability to brush aside bad encounters and continue serenely with his day, as though no one could possibly upset him. Perhaps he was practiced because he'd been raised to it, but I'd never learned the art of it, and doubted I ever would.

I RECEIVED WORD FROM LADY BRECKENRIDGE THE next morning that I could call on her, but when I arrived at her house in South Audley Street, the lady she had in her front sitting room was Mrs. Dale.

Annabelle Dale was much as Lady Breckenridge had described—red-rimmed eyes, past her first youth, thin and pale. She regarded me calmly, though her fingers twitched in her lap.

I was introduced, Lady Breckenridge and I sat down, and Barnstable brought coffee with cakes—an innocuous gathering. When Barnstable departed, Mrs. Dale set aside her cup and lifted her gaze to mine.

"Well, Captain Lacey. What did you wish to ask me?"

"I wanted to express my regret for the harm this incident has done," I said, "and to ask after Lady Clifford. Is she well?"

"She will recover. She has done this before, unfortunately. Living with his lordship is a great trial to her. He does everything to set us against each other." She smiled, and I could see that once, Annabelle Dale had been quite pretty. "It piques him that he cannot, not forever."

"But you and Lady Clifford must have had a bad quarrel," I said. "She was willing to accuse you of stealing her necklace."

"It is nothing we have not weathered before. I've known Marguerite since we were girls. She feels things too deeply and can become so easily jealous. She sought to punish me for . . . well, let us just say it was jealousy. And hurt. She sought to punish her husband, as well. Two in one blow."

"Then she felt remorse when Waters was arrested," I said. "But she was still angry at you, which is why she accused you to me. I think she hoped that I, with my reputation for running down criminals, could find an outside party on which to pin the crime. A known housebreaker or jewel thief. That person would be arrested, and you and Waters would be cleared."

Mrs. Dale pulled a handkerchief from her pocket, but she only clutched it between her fingers. "You have the right of it. Marguerite can be a fool sometimes. When you spoke to her at the musicale, she realized that you were unraveling her lies, and she panicked. She drank enough laudanum to make her dangerously ill, and of course Lord Clifford went to shout at Mr.

Grenville. Mr. Grenville would tell you to leave it alone, and all would be finished."

Lady Breckenridge, who sat with her elegant legs crossed, her cup held daintily, broke in. "Lady Clifford does not understand the captain, then. He is like a bulldog—does not let go once he sinks his teeth in. He will have the answer to the problem, no matter who does not wish him to find it."

I winced a little at her assessment, and she raised her brows at me over her cup.

"I realized that," Mrs. Dale said. "And so I felt you deserved the truth. Please understand, and leave Marguerite be, Captain. She was silly to approach Mr. Grenville in the first place, and now she is paying for her foolishness."

"I understand," I said. "Lady Clifford is a most unhappy woman, and she is lucky she has you to look after her." I leaned forward, resting my arms on my knees. "The necklace was never stolen, was it?"

Mrs. Dale glanced quickly at Lady Breckenridge. "I can hardly answer that."

"I have no interest in telling Lord Clifford," I said. "Neither, I am certain, has Lady Breckenridge. Yesterday, Clifford went so far as to try to assault Mr. Grenville in the park. My loyalty was never to him. It was Lady Clifford who asked for my help, and to Lady Clifford that I answer."

"And I am most discreet," Lady Breckenridge said. "You may tell Lady Clifford that she will remain on my guest list, no matter what happens. Clifford is a brute and a bully, and she deserves more than being her husband's creature." Which was one of the most generous things I'd ever heard Lady Breckenridge say about another woman.

"I am right, am I not?" I asked. "If the necklace truly has been stolen, then I will find it and the culprit. If not, I will leave it alone. But no search of your house, not by you and your servants or by Pomeroy and his patrollers has turned up the necklace. What became of it, Mrs. Dale?"

Mrs. Dale pulled a bit more on the handkerchief, and her face burned red. "I threw it into the Thames."

I stared at her. Lady Breckenridge quickly set down her porcelain cup. "Dear heavens," she said. "Why?"

"Marguerite asked me to. She hated the thing. She loves the little strand of diamonds her mother left her, but Lord Clifford has forbidden her to wear them, saying they are not prominent enough. Marguerite decided that if she pretended the large necklace had been stolen, she'd never have to see the bloody thing again. She had no way of knowing things would escalate into such a mess, that her husband would be goaded into hiring a Runner who would arrest poor Waters. Marguerite gave the necklace to me, and asked me to drop it into the river. So I did."

"Good Lord." Lady Breckenridge lifted her cup and took a large swallow of tea.

De la Fontaine's legacy, swimming in mud at the bottom of the Thames. "Mrs. Dale, you do know those diamonds were worth thousands of guineas, do you not?"

Annabelle Dale shrugged. "What is that compared

to peace, Captain Lacey? Thousands of guineas well spent, I think."

Her voice was calm, her hands quiet around her handkerchief. Mrs. Dale, stuck in the Clifford household, too poor to live on her own and subject to Lord Clifford's unwanted attentions, could have hidden the necklace, planning to use it to fund her way to freedom. But watching her, I didn't think she had. I saw understanding for Lady Clifford in her eyes, and fierce devotion.

This, in other words, was a gesture of love from Mrs. Dale and one of defiance by Lady Clifford. A gesture they could reveal to no one but themselves. The necklace had become a symbol of victory of two women over the man who held them in thrall.

"And then you quarreled," I said gently. "And in her burst of anger, she accused you of stealing the necklace. No proof, of course. Lady Clifford must not have truly believed you would be arrested, or at least did not think about it too much. Waters would not have been taken either, except that Pomeroy likes to arrest people. You then asked Lord Clifford to use his influence to save Waters."

Mrs. Dale nodded. "Marguerite was so fond of her, was so heartbroken, and of course Waters was entirely innocent. I have some little power with Lord Clifford, and so I used it."

"It was kind of you."

She met my gaze again. "Please leave it alone, Captain. Let her be at peace."

I nodded. How I would explain to de la Fontaine that his beloved family heirloom was at the bottom of the Thames, I did not know. Some waterman would find the necklace in the mud, years hence, and consider himself lucky. He'd either turn it in for a reward or try to keep it.

A strange ending to a strange problem.

"Thank you, Mrs. Dale, for being so candid," I said. "You may assure Lady Clifford that I understand and will cease with the matter altogether."

Mrs. Dale folded back into her seat and pressed her handkerchief to her mouth. "Thank you," she whispered. "Thank you."

When Barnstable had seen Mrs. Dale out, Lady Breckenridge rose and plucked a cigarillo from a box on the mantelpiece. She lit it with a spill from the fireplace and blew out a gray plume of smoke.

"You do like to keep your friends in the dark, Lacey. I had the wrong solution all this time. Why would Mrs. Dale do such an odd thing? She hasn't two coins to rub together—why not tuck the necklace under her cloak and run off with it? Gracious, I would have."

"I would have been tempted to do the same," I said. "But Mrs. Dale is devoted to Lady Clifford. Very much so. She'd never have left her alone to face Lord Clifford."

Lady Breckenridge drew again on the cigarillo, and her brows rose as she released the smoke. "It is like that, is it? I know now why Grenville grows so frustrated with you. You like to keep the most interesting tidbits to yourself."

"If I must."

She gave me a steady look. "Well, I will decide

whether to grow offended or to admire your integrity. But in the meantime I will call in another favor for my assistance on this problem. And no, I will not tell you what it is until time."

I saluted her with my teacup. "I will wait with anticipation."

"I highly doubt that." Lady Breckenridge smiled. "I will write when you are to call on me again, and then the balance might be paid. Now I must bid you good afternoon. So many things to do."

I had not thought to leave so soon, but I conceded that a dowager viscountess would have a full schedule during the high season. She softened the dismissal by kissing me again, this time pressing her lips to my mouth.

AND THAT, I THOUGHT, WAS THE END OF IT.

Lord Clifford still hung out a reward for the return of the necklace but made clear he wanted no one else in his household accused. Pomeroy continued to try to hunt down a thief, but because he could turn up no evidence of anyone else having taken the necklace, he soon moved to other, potentially more lucrative cases. I hadn't yet told de la Fontaine that his daughter's legacy had been tossed into the river, trying to decide how to impart this without betraying Lady Clifford.

Not half a week later, James Denis sent me a letter —brief and to the point—instructing me to pay him a visit. He'd send a carriage for me to avoid my excuses of not having enough shillings to pay my way across town.

I disliked obeying commands from Denis, but this time, I was interested in what he had to say. Denis's sumptuous coach carried me to Curzon Street, and once inside the house, I was ushered into his uncluttered study.

Denis waited, his hands folded on the blank surface of his desk while one of his pugilist footmen gestured me to an armchair and poured a glass of brandy for me. As soon as he and a second footmen took up their places—one at the door, one by the window—Denis spoke.

"I have found the diamond necklace belonging to de la Fontaine," he said.

My brows shot up. "Found it? Muddy, was it?"

Denis's eyes flickered, and for the first time since I'd met him, I sensed that I'd puzzled him.

"I located the necklace in France," he said.

"France?" My turn to be puzzled.

"In the possession of a minor aristocrat in the court of Louis XVIII. A minor aristocrat willing to give up the necklace for a fraction of its worth, because he was too ignorant to understand its value. According to his story, he bought the necklace from an Englishman in London three years ago and carried it back to France with him when the Bourbon king was restored to power."

My mind swam as I struggled to rearrange facts. "What Englishman? Clifford? Three years ago? He was certain?" But what then had Mrs. Dale thrown into the Thames?

"I had the necklace examined by a jeweler," Denis continued. "One of mine. He is the best in the business and quite reliable, I promise you. He proclaimed the diamonds real and the necklace de la Fontaine's. That means, Captain, that the stolen necklace you and Mr. Grenville have been chasing all over London is a copy, a paste replica. You have been led down the garden path."

"By whom? Clifford?"

"Assuredly, since he is the man who sold it to the Frenchman."

Bloody hell. No wonder Clifford had been so furious with Grenville and me for trying to find the necklace. Lady Clifford had made a fuss and gained the attention of Bow Street, but then Lord Clifford had done everything in his power to stop the investigation and deter Pomeroy. I wagered that Clifford didn't care two figs for how much we'd disturbed his household; he was only worried that we might reveal he'd been forced to sell his wife's jewels and humiliate him. Damn the man.

Denis opened a drawer, drew out the necklace, and laid it on a velvet cloth on top of his desk.

The diamonds glittered against the dark cloth, facets white and sharp blue in the candlelight. The center stone was the size of a robin's egg, perfectly cut from what I could see. The surrounding pieces, large diamonds encircled by smaller ones, were just as fine. I was no expert in jewels, but even the slowest person could see that this necklace was remarkable.

"It could be yours, Captain, if you wish it."

I lifted my eyes from it, entranced. "What on earth would I do with such a thing?"

"Sell it, give it to your lady, restore it to de la Fontaine . . . Whatever you like."

I sat back, my enchantment with the jewels gone. "For what price?"

"You are a resourceful man, Captain. I could use you, as I've told you before. Pledge yourself to me, and the necklace is yours." His voice held nothing, no emotion, his face, even less.

"You'd never believe I would agree to that, would you?" I asked.

"Not really." He nearly smiled, as close to amused as I'd ever seen him. "But I thought it worth a try." Denis closed the cloth over the magnificent diamonds and slid them back inside the drawer.

"That belongs to de la Fontaine," I said.

"De la Fontaine does not have the resources to buy the necklace back from me, nor does he have much to offer me in kind. He has cut off all ties to anyone who might be useful to me, preferring to live quietly in middleclass London with his daughter and grandchildren. He at least has found contentment with his family."

"Which is why you should return the necklace to him," I said in a hard voice. "He wishes to give it to his daughter."

Denis pressed his palms flat on his desk. "You have a strong sense of fairness, Captain, which is why I continually attempt to recruit you. I have not said I would not give the necklace to de la Fontaine. His son-in-law has a political bent. He hopes to win a seat in the House of Commons as soon as he can. Perhaps I can help him with such a thing."

Which meant that Denis would control that seat in Commons, and de la Fontaine's son-in-law would back any bill Denis wanted him to, vote the way Denis wanted him to—jump up and touch the ceiling whenever Denis wanted him to.

"For once, could you not do something out of benevolence?" I asked. "Imagine what such a gesture would do for your credibility."

Denis signaled to the pugilist at the door, who came forward. The interview was at an end. "I told you about the necklace as a courtesy, Captain. What I do with it is for me to decide. I imagine de la Fontaine will have it in the end."

"Leave him alone," I said with heat. "He has lost everything. Let him die in peace."

Denis's brows rose the slightest bit. "The Comte de la Fontaine used to be a great tyrant. He is one of the reasons the revolution in France began at all. He fled as soon as the tide began to turn, because he would have been among the first to the guillotine. The cry for his arrest had already gone out."

"He lost his only son, in our war."

"Fighting the republican bastards who drove him from his home," Denis said smoothly.

"Perhaps." I stood up, finding myself next to the pugilist who'd halted beside my chair. "But he's had to live thirty years in poverty in the damp of London, and is now a poor relation to his rather thick English son-in-law. That is enough of a punishment for any man, do you not think?"

Again, the look of near amusement. "As you say, Captain. I will keep you informed. Good day."

I KNEW DENIS WANTED ME TO BE GRATEFUL TO HIM for bothering to tell me about the necklace at all. He also wanted to rub my face in the fact that he'd used everything I'd done in my investigation to further his own wealth and power.

He might be right that de la Fontaine had possessed the same kind of arrogant ruthlessness that Denis himself had now. But the world turned, and it changed, and eventually all tyrants fell to become dust.

I wrote to de la Fontaine, telling him that Denis had the necklace, and suggested he apply to a magistrate I knew who was not in Denis's network. I then wrote to the magistrate in question, informing Sir Montague Harris of all that had happened, though I kept silent on the roles Mrs. Dale and Lady Clifford had played in the necklace's loss. After all, they'd only disposed of an inexpensive copy.

I had no way of knowing whether de la Fontaine would act against Denis or end up bargaining with him. Or perhaps drop the matter altogether.

I somehow did not think he'd choose the last recourse, and I was correct. Several days later, Sir Montague replied to me, saying that he'd spoken to de la Fontaine, but that de la Fontaine had not wanted to prosecute either Denis or Lord Clifford.

I received a letter from de la Fontaine himself soon after that. In it he thanked me for my assistance, told me that the necklace had been returned to him, and made a vague suggestion that perhaps we might share fine brandy again one day. Nothing more. Not until months later did I see his son-in-law stand for Parliament and be elected by a landslide. James Denis had won again.

For now, I was finished with the business. I tied the last two threads of the affair the day after I received de la Fontaine's letter. The first came in the form of a note from Lady Breckenridge, calling in her favor and bidding me to attend her at her home.

CHAPTER 10

S uch a delight," Lady Breckenridge said. "Captain Lacey answers a summons. I hear from Grenville that you do not always comply."

She'd received me in her sitting room, she wearing a deep blue afternoon dress, its décolletage trimmed with light blue ribbon woven through the darker cloth. The ribbon matched the bandeau in her hair and brought out the blue of her eyes.

She did not invite me to sit down. We stood near the fireplace, the heat from the coals soaking into my bones. I leaned on the walking stick she'd given me, its handle warm under my palm.

"I can be abominably rude at times," I said.

Lady Breckenridge shrugged, her shrugs as smooth and practiced as Denis's own. "You do not rush to obey those who seek to command you. Your independence makes people puzzle over you."

I gave her a wry smile. "They puzzle over why a

poor nobody does not hasten to snatch from every hand."

"Your behavior does give others something to talk about, Lacey."

"Including you, my lady."

Her gaze went cool. "I admit to the curiosity, but I choose very carefully to whom I speak about what."

I believed her. "I beg your pardon," I said. "I was teasing and meant no censure. You have invited me here to call in your favor. Perhaps you should tell me what it is."

She smiled. "Have done with it, you mean? I can imagine you wondering like mad what I would ask of you as you rode over from Covent Garden. But you may cease worrying. The task is very simple. I wish for you to meet my son."

I blinked in surprise. I'd never met Lady Brecken-ridge's son, who would be about five by now. The young Viscount Breckenridge stayed with his grandmother in the country much of the time, so I had been told, tucked away with nannies and tutors and other caretakers.

Lady Breckenridge seldom spoke of the boy, but observing her now, I realized that her silence was not because she had no affection for him. I saw in her the same thing I'd seen in Marianne during the Sudbury School problem—a woman who loved desperately and protected fiercely.

I gave her another half bow. "I would be honored, my lady."

"Very well, then." She turned from me in a brush of faint perfume and tugged on a bell pull. When the

ever-efficient Barnstable glided in, she said, "Tell
Nanny to bring Peter downstairs."

"You mean you wish me to meet him now?" I
asked. "He is here?"

Barnstable had already disappeared to carry out his
lady's wishes. "Before you can change your mind," she
said. "Shall we?"

She slid her hand into the crook of my arm and
more or less forced me to guide her out of the room.

The staircase hall of Lady Breckenridge's house
was plastered in pale colors, with niches holding vases
of hothouse flowers. Paintings from centuries past
hung on the walls—originals, not copies. Wide stairs
with a polished railing ran up into the dim recesses of
the house.

I heard a door shut high above us. In a few
moments, two people came down the stairs: a tall,
slender woman in neat black, and a small lad for whom
the black-clad nanny slowed her steps.

The boy's suit was a miniature of what Grenville
would wear, down to the pantaloons and well-shined
pumps. However, Viscount Breckenridge would never
attain Grenville's taut slimness. He had a sturdiness
that spoke of developing muscle, and in a dozen or so
years, he would attain the large, powerful build of his
father.

The lad stopped a few stairs above me and stared
with undisguised curiosity. I was in my regimentals,
my braid neatly fastened, my unruly hair somewhat
tamed, my boots as polished as Bartholomew could
make them. I saw the lad take note of my height, the
breadth of my shoulders, my bearing, my uniform.

"This is Peter," Lady Breckenridge said, a note of pride in her voice. "Peter, this is Captain Lacey, my friend I have mentioned."

Peter was inclined to do nothing but stare, but at a surreptitious nudge from his nanny, he bowed correctly. "How do you do?" he asked.

He was far too polite for a lad of five. He ought to be tearing up and down the stairs and shouting at the top of his voice. But perhaps he'd been persuaded to be on his best behavior for me—either that or I'd stunned the lad.

I made a formal bow. "How do you do, Your Lordship."

I'd never been one to seek the company of children, except for my daughter, but I decided that a brief smile was called for. Young Viscount Breckenridge grinned back at me then quickly hid it.

A pang bit my heart. My daughter and I had exchanged such covert smiles when we were supposed to be formal and serious, knowing we'd both be scolded if caught. I missed her with an ache that had never subsided.

"Do you ride?" I found myself asking the boy.

"Yes, sir." The small voice held a scoff, as though I were an idiot for asking. He was a lordship after all, born to horse and hound.

"Perhaps your mother will allow you to ride with me in the park sometime. I have some modest skill."

"Will you show me how to ride like a cavalryman?" The scorn vanished, and Peter sounded like a normal, eager boy.

I glanced at Lady Breckenridge, but she looked in

no way dismayed. She went to Peter and took his hands. "If you are good, darling. Now give me a kiss good night."

Peter obeyed, and I was pleased to see that he kissed his mother with affection. There was no strain between Lady Breckenridge and her son.

Introductions over, Peter was taken his slow way back upstairs with nanny. He glanced back down at me over the banisters but did nothing so undignified as wave. I gave him another friendly nod, and he continued climbing, seeking his nursery once more.

I turned to Lady Breckenridge. "Have I fulfilled my obligation?"

The smile she gave me eased some of the hurt in my heart, enough to make me believe that the pain could be assuaged a bit were I often enough in her presence.

"Excellently well, Captain," Lady Breckenridge said. She touched my arm again, her fingers warm.

I dared lift her hand to my lips. "I am pleased to hear it, my lady," I said.

THE LAST THREAD OF THE NECKLACE AFFAIR WAS tied when I accepted Grenville's invitation to dine at Watier's that night. Watier's, famous for food provided by chefs of the Prince Regent, offered the deepest gaming in London. Games of macao and whist relieved gentlemen of their fortunes in one room, while the dining room provided excellent cuisine with which to ease the sting.

Grenville was in full dress that evening, which

meant that he wore a suit so tailored to his figure that he might have been poured into it. Pantaloons that emphasized his muscular calves were buttoned at the ankle above fine leather pumps. His quizzing glass hung on a fine gold chain, ever ready for scrutinizing the gauche.

After we'd finished our excellent meal and looked in on the games room, I was dismayed to see Lord Clifford making so bold as to approach us. A few of the dandies looked up with interest when Clifford walked to Grenville and put a hand on his shoulder.

Grenville glanced disdainfully at the large hand on his immaculate frock coat, but Clifford did not notice the censure. He let go only after he'd turned Grenville away from the crowd.

"I want to thank you, Grenville," Lord Clifford said.

"Do you?" Grenville's voice was icy. "Whatever for?"

"For agreeing to stay out of my business. Decent of you."

I suppressed my sudden urge to punch the man, but this time it was Grenville who took retribution. He stepped back one pace, lifted his quizzing glass, and studied Clifford through it.

"Let me see," Grenville said. "You stole an extremely valuable necklace from a wretched French émigré who was trying to remove his family from the dangers of France. A necklace you later sold—probably for a fraction of its worth—to cover your debts, whatever they were, giving your wife a copy so she wouldn't guess what you'd done. Then, when the false necklace goes missing and Lady Clifford seeks our help, you harass and browbeat her so much that she attempts to take her own life. All the while betraying her with her closest friend and companion, the only comfort she has. I'd say there was not much decent in the entire business."

Clifford flushed. "I told you, Grenville, what goes on in a man's household has nothing to do with you."

"Oh, but it has. Your wife reached out to me and Captain Lacey, because she had nowhere else to turn. And you may be correct that your household is your business, but the fact remains that you stole the diamonds from de la Fontaine in the first place. Not very sporting of you. In fact, one might call that a crime."

"Fontaine was hated among the French," Clifford said. "They'd applaud me."

"Ah, you are a latter-day Robin Hood, stealing from the corrupt rich to give to the . . . well, to yourself. And then to sell them and drape your wife in paste diamonds. Dear me." Grenville shook his head.

We had the attention of much of the room. Though we spoke in low voices, Grenville's attitude of derision spoke volumes.

"I had to sell them," Clifford said. "I'd promised Derwent a large sum for his damned reforms and then had some bad luck at games. I sold the necklace to pay my debts and not leave Derwent standing. Would have made me a laughingstock. Nothing else to be done."

"You might have explained to your wife," I said. "You ought to have trusted her with the truth."

"Damn it, Lacey, you've met my wife. You know

what she is. She would never be able to keep her damn fool mouth shut. She'd blab all to her blasted companion, upon whom she's much too dependent. A wife should know who is master, after all."

So, he'd taken Mrs. Dale to his bed to keep Lady Clifford under his thumb. A man who ruled his household by manipulation, lies, and fear. How was he better than a French aristocrat who'd made a hundred peasants labor for him?

He wasn't. De la Fontaine had risked all and given up everything to take his children out of danger. Even after it had been safe for him to return home, de la Fontaine had stayed in his reduced circumstances to be with his one remaining child and his grandchildren.

Grenville's look turned to one of unfeigned disgust. He sniffed, lowered his quizzing glass, adjusted his gloves, and said, "I believe, Lord Clifford, that I will have to disapprove of you."

"What the devil does that mean? Why should I care whether you approve or disapprove of anything I do?"

Lord Clifford did not realize his danger, but I knew quite well what Grenville meant. Clifford might be an earl, but such was the power of Lucius Grenville in the fashionable world that if he wanted a man to be cut, that man would be cut. *One can be an earl,* I could imagine Lady Breckenridge saying in her clear, acerbic tones, *and still be invited nowhere.*

Grenville did not wait. There, in the very crowded gaming rooms of Watier's, with one movement of his slim shoulders, with one spin on his immaculate heels, Grenville turned his back on Lord Clifford, and ruined him.

THE DISAPPEARANCE OF MISS SARAH OSWALD

THE DISAPPEARANCE OF MISS SARAH OSWALD

LONDON, 1817

*L*ondon swallowed people whole. It had swallowed me. It had swallowed Thaddeus Oswald, MP. It had swallowed Thaddeus Oswald's daughter, and now he expected me to find her.

Oswald told me about his daughter in a coffee house in Pall Mall late one afternoon, in a room that reeked of scalded coffee and cheroot smoke. His daughter, sent to London to live with her aunt, was now lost, gone, vanished into the city.

There wasn't much hope, he said. Either she was dead or beyond redemption.

"My sister searched and gave up," Oswald told me, looking tired and ashamed. "My son even posted a reward, but nothing came of it."

"That was eight months ago," I said. "Why approach me now?"

Oswald twisted his coffee cup on its saucer as he invented an explanation for why he'd waited so long. "I met Brandon over cards last night," he said. "Hadn't seen him in a donkey's age. Brandon said that if anyone could find out the truth, it would be you."

Brandon had been my colonel during the Peninsular War. He was the man responsible for my career in the army, for saving my life, and for the destruction of my leg that had forced me to resign. Our current relations had become more cordial of late but remained stiff. Brandon did not much approve of my habit of running all over London hunting criminals, but he conceded that I'd had success in the past.

Oswald had given up finding his daughter, I surmised, but Colonel Brandon, who could rally the most dejected of men, had persuaded him to try one final time. So he'd sent Oswald to me, but I could see that Oswald had already tired of hope.

"How old is you daughter, Mr. Oswald?"

"She would have been eighteen in April," Oswald said and started to cry.

In my rooms above the pastry shop near Covent Garden, I stripped to my skin and stood before the fire, letting it bake the chill from my bones. I studied the drawing of Sarah Oswald her father had given me before we parted—one of the reward notices his son had posted. It showed a smiling girl with dark curls wearing a close-fitting white cap. She looked the same as many other girls of her age, rich or poor, gentry or working class.

What had happened was probably very simple.

Procuresses met coaches from the country and enticed away lone girls with promises of honest employment or places to stay. The girls ended up in nunneries or walking the streets or as the private playthings of upper-class gentlemen. Some were lucky and thrived, but many, many more found their way to the work-houses and death.

Whorehouse or workhouse, I did not think Sarah's family wanted her back. They were upright, middle-class people who would view shame as a fate worse than death — best to sweep it far away and out of sight. But Brandon had shown Oswald a way to put his mind at rest — let Captain Lacey find out whether she's alive or dead. Captain Lacey was good at finding things out.

Things I'd found out in the army had cost me my health, my career, and most of my sanity, and had cast me onto the uncaring shores of London — a worn out, forty-odd, ex-captain of King George's cavalry who now had to hobble about with a walking stick. A hero from the Peninsular Wars against Boney the Bastard.

I extinguished my candles, pulled my linen night-shirt over my head, and crawled into bed. What lay before me was an impossible task, and I was curious enough and stupid enough to attempt it.

Miss Clothilde Oswald, Sarah's aunt, lived in a house near Portman Square. The drawing room I found myself in at ten the next morning was neither ostentatious nor spare, but a balance that said *I have money but spend it wisely.*

Miss Oswald gave the same impression. Her neat, rather plain costume of lilac gown, gray jacket, and silk cap spoke of both modesty and expense.

She'd brought a companion with her, a woman in the dull clothes of a lady's drudge. The companion darted nervous glances at me then went to the corner by the fire and took up some needlework. A woman unused to men, I decided.

"Captain Gabriel Lacey?" Miss Oswald waved me to a chair then watched me sharply, as though certain I'd turn into a wild beast and ravish her and her companion together. I've been told that men do that.

"My brother said you wanted to ask about Sarah, but I do not know what more I can tell you. That was eight months ago, and we've heard nothing."

I understood. As far as Miss Oswald was concerned, Sarah was gone, and that was the end of it.

"Mr. Oswald told me that you were late to collect your niece at the coaching inn because of some altercation among your staff," I said.

"Yes, I remember distinctly. The cook had bought oysters for dinner and Miss Rice . . ." Miss Oswald cast a disparaging glance at her companion . . . "thought they were off and should not be served. The cook believed Miss Rice to be wrong, and they began a merry argument."

"And you went down to settle it?"

"I was forced to. It was very silly. When in doubt, throw it out, is my motto. No doubt miss Rice was correct. She is not given to fancies and hysteria."

Miss Rice glanced up from her corner, rather like a dog hearing itself being discussed. When Miss Rice caught my eye, she turned fiery red and hastily bent over her needlework again.

"By the time I'd settled the argument, it was a half hour past when I should have left for the coaching inn. I made all haste, but I was too late. Sarah was gone. Foolish girl. Why she hadn't waited for me, when she knew I was coming, I'll never know."

"And you made inquiries?" Oswald had told me, but I wanted to hear the story from her lips.

"To be certain I did. I asked the coachman if she'd been on the coach at all, and he assured me that she had. I did not like the look of him, but he seemed guilty of nothing more than drinking too much gin on the road. I asked the hostler and innkeeper and everyone who happened to be in the yard. No one noticed a thing. Useless of them."

"Your brother said that the hostler's boy saw her."

"Yes. After a few shillings, he told me that Sarah — or a girl who looked like Sarah — had gone away with a woman in a white cap and black cloak. He had the effrontery to claim that the woman looked like me."

"Perhaps she did," I offered, "and Sarah mistook her for you at first, not having seen you since she was a very small child. Or perhaps the woman told Sarah she would take her to you. Perhaps she looked quite respectable. From what your brother says of Sarah, it's doubtful she'd have gone off with a questionable stranger of her own volition."

"Sarah was nearly eighteen," Miss Oswald said impatiently. "No doubt the woman promised her a bit of jewelry or a fan or some frippery. Sarah was unhappy that she was to stay with me when she came to London. She wanted suitors and balls and operas, not sensible lessons."

As most eighteen-year-old girls would. Many young women were already married by eighteen, and Sarah might have begun to worry about being left on the shelf. "Sarah did not travel alone, did she? She must have had a maid or other servant with her, at least."

Miss Oswald sniffed. "Her maid became ill and could not accompany her. Sarah's father hired another girl to go with her at the last minute. Shiftless thing. Ran away as soon as they disembarked, the hostler's boy told me."

"Where do you think Sarah is now, Miss Oswald?"

She gave me a look. "Come, Captain, you and I both know. I am a spinster, but I'm not naive. Even if Sarah is alive, she'll be utterly ruined."

I got to my feet. "Thank you for seeing me, Miss Oswald. I will send word if I discover anything."

"No need. My niece is dead, Captain Lacey. Let her remain so."

"I OFFERED FIVE GUINEAS FOR ANY INFORMATION regarding my sister," Robert Oswald said. "Nothing came of it."

Robert Oswald was a year down from Oxford and full of himself. He wore rouge and too much scent, and his collar points were so high he could not turn his head.

I met Robert that evening at a sporting house

where we watched two women in scanty clothing box each other. I impressed young Mr. Oswald by winning a few pounds on the fight, then we adjourned to a coffee house in St. James's where I further impressed him by beating him at cards.

"And you have no idea where she might have gone?" I asked.

"Oh, I have an idea, as we all do. There's nothing to be done about it, and Father knows it. I rather believe he hopes she's dead."

"Do you believe she's dead?"

Robert shrugged. "Doesn't matter, does it? If Sarah were all right, she'd have seen the handbills and found me, wouldn't she? Or written."

"Why did not you or your father go to Bow Street and hire a Runner?"

"Damnation!" This was not addressed to me; Robert glared up at a young man who'd jostled him in passing. "Watch what you're doing, Godwin."

"If you didn't sit half out of your chair, Oswald . . ."

Robert's mouth thinned to a hard, white line. "If you wish to settle this with pistols, I will."

The other young man gave him a withering look. "No need. I beg your pardon."

He walked on. Robert returned to the game. "Beetle-brained oaf." He played a card, his face flushed, his breathing rapid.

I reminded him of my question about Bow Street.

Robert had to lay down a few more cards before he was calm enough to answer. "I did go round to Bow Street, as a matter of fact, though I never told m'father. A Runner spoke to me. He was rude and insulting, but he told me what I already knew. She's either become a tart, or she's dead. Either way, there is not much we can do, is there?" Robert jotted down points. "The devil, Lacey, you win again. You have cursed good luck tonight. Another?"

THE NEXT AFTERNOON, I WENT TO THE COACHING inn, but I found no new information there. The hostler's boy told me exactly what he'd told Clothilde Oswald, that Sarah had gone off with a respectable-looking woman in a white cap. The offer of a few shillings produced no more information.

I did not find the coachman. The innkeeper informed me that the man had died in an accident a few weeks before on the Great North Road. I recalled what Miss Oswald had said about gin and was not very surprised.

It was quiet in the yard and outside in the street, between arrivals of the coaches from the south. The inn's gray walls reached to the damp gray sky, the only bit of color being the girl who lounged against one wall, her curls an artificial red. She wore virginal white and a threadbare cloak of dark blue, but in this drab setting, she looked as colorful as a butterfly.

On the off chance, I showed her the drawing of Sarah.

"Yeah, I know her," she surprised me by saying. "You her dad?"

"A friend of her family," I improvised. "Do you know where I can find her?"

"Suppose so. She's one of Ma Martin's."

"Who is Ma Martin?" I asked, trying to suppress hope.

The girl shrugged. "Everyone knows her. Her house ain't far."

Then why hadn't the hostler's boy recognized her? I glanced at the closed door of the stable yard, and the girl gave a little laugh.

"Did they tell you they'd never seen her? Course they did. She pays 'em to keep their mouths shut."

I ought to have guessed. "Will you show me this house?"

"I could, but the girl in this picture ain't there no more."

My hopes faded. "Do you happen to know where she went?"

The girl's gaze drifted down my bad left leg. "Does it pain you?"

"It does," I said. "Especially in the damp."

She straightened up, turning the full charm of her large brown eyes on me. "You come with me then. I'll tell you all about it inside, once we get you warm." She grinned. "Promise."

I KNEW FULL WELL THAT THE YOUNG WOMAN COULD lead me away and try to rob me, possibly with cohorts waiting in her rooms. I went with her regardless, not wanting to miss some vital bit of information about Sarah. Besides, I had little to steal.

She led me down a tiny lane to a faded door that

opened right onto the cobbles. Behind the door, a narrow stair went up between walls covered with faded paper to a room bare of all furniture except a low bed with a moth-eaten coverlet.

The girl hung up her cloak and stirred the fire on the small hearth to life. "Sit yerself down. And let Frances take care of yer."

I limped to the bed and lowered myself to it. I couldn't hide my grunt of pain as my knee bent. It did feel good to take my weight from it.

Frances knelt in front of me and slid my boot from my left foot. I winced when she seized my stiff knee, but she started to knead the muscles, her hands warm and strong.

I leaned back and let her have her way with me.

"Do you know where Sarah is?" I asked, a bit breathily.

Frances smiled, showing crooked teeth. "You said you were her friend. Does that mean you fancy her?"

"I said I was a friend of the *family*. Her father is worried about her."

"I ask, because she didn't much like men. She told me she hated them." Frances winked. "Not like me. I like a gentleman just fine."

"Why did Sarah leave Ma Martin's? Did she manage to run away?"

Frances continued to rub my knee, my muscles relaxing beneath her skilled touch. "She didn't need to run away. Someone came in a carriage and took her away. A fine coach, it was. She's got someone to look after her now."

I saw my task grow impossible again. "Then you do

not know where she is."

"I never said that. She's in Clark Street."

I sat up quickly and sucked in a breath as pain shot through my knee. I put my hands over Frances's, stilling her distracting massage.

"Do you know who this man was?" I asked. "Did you recognize the carriage? Had he come to Ma Martin's before?"

"No," Frances said, and I whispered, "Damn."

Frances grinned. "Fooled you, didn't I? It weren't a man. It were a lady."

I stared. "A lady?"

"A lady from Clark Street. She came back to fetch Sarah's things and told Ma Martin to send the rest to Clark Street. I never heard where in Clark Street, though. Must be one of those good works people. The kind I hides from." Frances winked. "Have I helped?"

"You have. You have helped very much. You've given me a place to start."

"I meant about your leg."

"That as well." I flexed my knee. The ache had subsided, and the joint felt loose and warm.

"Good. Want me to rub something else?"

A few years ago, I would have smiled and wiled away the rest of the afternoon with this warm young woman in her cozy little room.

"I have a lady," I said gently.

"And I have a man. But he knows what I am."

No doubt he did. I dug into my pockets and emptied it of the coins I'd won from Robert Oswald the night before. I left myself a few shillings to pay hackney drivers and gave the rest to Frances.

Frances's eyes widened at the money on her palm. "Well, ain't you the generous one? And all I did was fondle your knee."

I kissed her forehead. "You have made me ever so much better," I said and left her.

CLARK STREET, NOT FAR FROM THE HEART OF banking London, held a double row of respectable middleclass houses that curved away from where I stood.

I'd arrived in time to see the married gentlemen of the neighborhood—clerks, bankers, and barristers—return home to wives and children. I made careful note of their house numbers and dismissed these. I doubted any wife, no matter how charitable, would let a street girl into a house with her husband.

That left about fifteen houses on the crescent for me to try. I milled along, passing the time with peddlers and vendors, trying with my questions to narrow the number further still.

Five of the fifteen houses, I learned, were occupied by elderly gentlemen, five by single gentlemen of independent means, and five by widows or spinsters and their companions.

At seven o'clock, I took a card from my pocket and wrote on its back with a stub of drawing pencil, "Would be pleased to speak with you regarding Sarah Oswald," and made to approach the doors of the widows and spinsters.

At the first two houses I was turned away by rude

young footmen, one of whom kicked away my cane. I gave him a look as I retrieved it that sent him scuttling to the safety of his vestibule.

At the third house, a maid took the card, disappeared with it, and returned after an agonizing quarter of an hour to admit me and bid me follow her upstairs.

The maid ushered me into a cheerful drawing room that held nothing luxurious or stylish. The furniture had a worn, comfortable look, and the fire grate was brightly polished—the room of someone who loved living in it.

A woman rose from an armless chair before the fire as I entered. She was about forty, thin and plain, but her watery blue eyes looked kind.

"Captain Lacey," she said. "I am Miss Sandington. Will you sit? How may I assist you?"

I took the chair she indicated, and she resumed her seat. "If you know anything about Sarah Oswald," I said, "please tell me. Her father is very worried about her."

"So he might well be. I will speak plainly, Captain. Sarah is here, but she will not leave."

Elation and relief chased through me—*Found, by God*—followed by puzzlement. "Is that your stipulation or hers?" I asked.

"Neither. Sarah is dying. She will likely not recover."

Miss Sandington spoke unwaveringly, but as the last word faded, so did her resolve. Her thin face crumpled, and tears flooded her eyes.

"Forgive me, Captain," she said, wiping her cheeks with her fingertips. "Sarah is very dear to me."

I offered her my handkerchief then sat silently and let her cry, knowing that finally I'd found someone who gave a damn about Sarah. A small clock ticked on the mantel as we sat, tiny slices of time.

When Miss Sandington had recovered somewhat, I resumed my questions. "How did Sarah come to stay with you? Did you discover her at Mrs. Martin's?"

She looked up, anger replacing sorrow. "So you know about that woman? I could not let Sarah go back to her. Sarah had been an innocent until that awful abbess got hold of her. I decided that Sarah could stay here, that I could look after her."

"It was kind of you."

Miss Sandington flushed. "No, Captain. It was not only kindness. I fell in love with Sarah Oswald." She smiled, but the smile did not reach her eyes. "Have I shocked you?"

"No," I said. "Surprised me, rather."

"Sarah is a sweet-tempered, very pretty girl, and I am an old fool."

She gave me a savage look but also a proud one. She would not apologize for her feelings.

"Will you tell me what happened?" I asked.

"I will tell you everything. You may go back to her father and repeat the story, so he can know what he has done to her. Mr. Oswald sent Sarah to her aunt in the first place, because Sarah refused to marry at his wish, to some country farmer twice her age. Sarah went with Mrs. Martin because that devil woman convinced Sarah that she'd have a job in a respectable shop, where she might meet a fine and handsome gentleman of means. Sarah thought this would suit her better than purgatory with her aunt. She had no way of knowing what Mrs. Martin was, poor lamb."

"And how did Sarah come to meet you?"

"A gentleman friend of mine sometimes finds . . . company . . . for me. He saw Sarah and thought she would suit me. I liked her at once; she was pretty and affectionate, and she told me she actually preferred . . . our way of doing things.

"The next day, she cried and clung to me and begged me not to send her back. She'd told me her story, and I had no intention of returning her to Mrs. Martin. I went to the house myself to collect her things and tell Mrs. Martin exactly what I thought." Her long fingers twitched in her lap, and she folded them into her palms. "That was six months ago."

"When did Sarah become ill?" I asked gently.

"Oh, she is not ill, Captain."

I stared in surprise. "You said she was dying."

"She is. But not from illness." Miss Sandington stood. "Come with me, Captain. I will show you."

I got to my feet and followed Miss Sandington out of the room and up another flight of stairs. She took me to a bedroom, which was dark but for one candle on a chest of drawers. When Miss Sandington lit another candle, I saw Sarah Oswald.

She reclined on a chaise, propped up on pillows that overflowed onto the floor. A bright quilt covered her to her neck, and the dark curls I'd seen peeping from her cap in the drawing now tumbled in a swath to her lap.

"There," Miss Sandington said, raising the candle high. "Go back and tell her father about *this*."

Sarah's face was no longer the sweet, fresh one of the drawing. Someone had smashed it, smashed it so the planes of her face had altered and flattened and were covered with dark bruises. Her mouth was open, and ragged, moist breathing came from between her lips. Her hands in her lap, tangled in her long hair, were twisted and broken.

Miss Sandington touched Sarah's shoulder, very gently, and pressed a kiss to the top of her head. "Sarah, darling," she whispered.

Sarah's eyes flicked open. She looked dully up at me, swept her gaze to Miss Sandington, and closed her eyes again.

"Good God," I said. "Who did this to her?"

"I do not know." Miss Sandington kissed Sarah again, straightened, and turned to me. "A week ago, she went out, not saying where, and was hours late coming home. I grew frantic, but she made it back here somehow. I found her on the scullery stairs, like this. A surgeon has tried to help her, but he is not optimistic."

"Can she not speak?"

"She has not said a word since she returned. Most of the time, she simply sleeps." Tears filled Miss Sandington's eyes once again.

I looked down at the broken, thin body that had once belonged to a robust girl. Sarah had been harmless, innocent, moved about by people who cared nothing for her happiness. Here, in Miss Sandington's home, she had at last found a haven, but someone had destroyed her even then.

I would discover who, and I would make them pay.

"What was she wearing the day this happened?"

I asked.

Miss Sandington gave me a blank look. "Her dress was in shreds and her cloak was ruined. We threw them away."

"Did she have a reticule, or a pocket? She might have had something with her that showed where she'd gone that day, or who she'd seen."

Miss Sandington shook her head. "The maid who helped me put her to bed would have put anything she found in the dressing table."

"May I?"

Miss Sandington nodded, and I went to the dressing table. Its surface was cluttered with ribbons and lace, combs and inexpensive jewelry, the frippery that Clothilde Oswald had so condemned. I found scraps of paper in the drawer: a fragment from a newspaper announcing an exhibition at Egyptian House, a list of popular novels, and receipt from a chocolate shop.

I glanced back at Miss Sandington. She sat on a straight-backed chair pulled to the chaise and was bent over Sarah's inert body. I slipped papers into my pocket, stood up, and quietly thanked Miss Sandington for telling me the tale.

She said good-bye to me, her eyes holding the blankness of sorrow, and I departed.

LACEY," ROBERT OSWALD GREETED ME AS I MET HIM going into the door of his lodgings. "Come upstairs and let me take my revenge. I have cards and brandy."

"No, thank you. I have come to tell you what I've discovered about your sister."

Robert's smile vanished, and he led me quickly up the stairs to a first-floor flat.

A thin, worried-looking man opened the door to us. Robert stripped off his gloves and tossed them at him, and the man fumbled and dropped them.

"Impudence." Robert retrieved the gloves himself, slapped the servant with them, and shoved him out of the room. "Sit down, Lacey, and tell me about it. You look grave. Is Sarah dead?"

I remained standing. "Your sister is alive," I said. "But she's been beaten so badly, it's doubtful she'll live."

Robert's eyes widened, and he dropped onto a soiled damask chair. "Beaten? By, er, one of her men, do you mean?"

"I spoke with the woman who is looking after her. Sarah hasn't been able to tell her who hurt her."

"The devil," Robert said. "What woman? Where is she?"

I drew out a paper I'd taken from Sarah's dressing table, unfolded it, and handed it to Robert. "I found that with Sarah's things."

The paper was one of the handbills showing the drawing of Sarah and offering a reward of five guineas for knowledge of her whereabouts. Robert stared at it as though he'd never seen it before.

I said, "Sarah found that and came to you, did she not? She came to tell you that she was well and happy and living with someone who loved her. Why did you not report to your family that you'd found her? And why did you lie to me?"

Robert stared at the drawing a moment longer and then up at me. "Well, Good God man, is it not obvious why? Because I did not want you to find her. Since you've discovered her anyway, damn you, very well then. She did come to me. But is it not better that my parents think her dead than where she is?"

"With Miss Sandington? With a woman who cares for her?"

Robert came out of his chair. "Sarah told me all about her relations with that—that *woman*. Dear God, a man's own sister."

"So you became angry with her," I said, my words cold. "And you beat her, just as you would your servant. But she was a young girl, no match for your strength. And in your temper you did not stop beating her."

Robert paled. "You do not know that."

"No, I am guessing. But I believe I've guessed right."

Robert flung himself away from me and began pacing. "Yes, yes, I did hit her. I was disgusted with her. But I did not think I'd hurt her that much."

"I am certain you did not mean to when you started. But I saw her."

"You have no proof, Lacey."

"No."

Robert swung to me. "Bloody hell, man. I could not help myself, could I? Imagine if she were your sister."

I only watched him. Robert's rage faded to worry. "Will you tell my father?"

"I have not decided," I said.

Robert seized my arm. "For God's sake, Lacey. You have no *proof*."

"Let go of me," I said. "You make me sick."

Robert let his hands drop to his sides, and I turned and made for the door, leaning heavily on my walking stick. The effects of Frances's massage had faded, and my knee pained me once more.

Behind me, Robert bleated, "Do you not see, Lacey, that it is better this way? If Sarah dies, she can no longer shame us, or herself."

I turned back. What Robert saw on my face was enough to make him cower, but he did not run. He must not have thought a crippled man was much of a threat.

He was wrong. My fist caught him full in the face. Scarlet blood gushed from his nose, and he clapped his hand to it as my next blow, with my cane, landed on his gut. Robert fell to his knees.

I left him there, huddled on his carpet, screaming for his servant. I closed the door and went down the stairs and out into the grimy, fog-shrouded city. St. James's was crowded, but I pushed through the throng, seeing no one, walking and walking until I had to stop in exhaustion.

I FOUND MYSELF AFTER A TIME OUTSIDE THE HOUSE of my lady love, on South Audley Street. Lady Breckenridge had gone out for the evening, but her ever-efficient butler, Barnstable, let me in, fed me brandy, and tended to my bruised knuckles and worn-out knee without asking questions. I sat in Lady Breckenridge's elegant little back parlor and breathed in her scent until I felt more at peace.

The next day, I walked from my rooms the short distance to Bow Street and told the Runner called Pomeroy all about Robert Oswald. Milton Pomeroy had been my loud, boisterous sergeant in the army, and now he was a large, boisterous Runner. He brightened at the prospect of a possible conviction.

Robert Oswald had been correct, however, when he'd accused me of having no proof. If Sarah did not recover and tell her story, there would be nothing to say that Robert had beaten her nearly to death. I doubted that Robert's servant would be brave enough to confess it, if he'd even witnessed it.

Pomeroy, on the other hand, did not bother with such trivialities. He went forth to arrest Robert Oswald, but did not find him. Robert disappeared from London, never to return. Pomeroy searched for him a while, then gave him up as not worth the trouble. There were far more lucrative criminals to pursue.

I never learned whether Sarah Oswald lived or died. I returned to Miss Sandington after a time to inquire how she was, to find that Miss Sandington's household had gone, moved to the country, so a coffee vendor thought. However, I did not read of Sarah's death in any newspaper, and from that day to this, I hoped she'd found her peace with Miss Sandington at last.

I never saw Robert Oswald again, and Thaddeus Oswald shunned me publicly thereafter.

THE GENTLEMAN'S
WALKING STICK

THE GENTLEMAN'S WALKING STICK

On a rainy morning in 1817, I visited Bond Street to purchase a bauble for my lady.

I gazed at trays of glittering jewels in the shop I entered and dreamed of adorning Lady Breckenridge with the best of them. I knew, however, that my captain's half-pay would allow me only the simplest of trinkets. The proprietor knew it too and abandoned me for the more prosperous-looking patrons who walked in behind me.

"Is it Captain Lacey?" a male voice rang out. "Jove, it is, as I live and breathe."

I turned to see a man of thirty-odd, his light brown hair damp with rain, favoring me with a familiar and hearty grin. In spite of the weather, his clothing was impeccable, from his pantaloons and polished Hessians to a fashionably tied cravat. An equally well-dressed older gentleman I didn't know stood behind him with a matron and a young woman with red-gold hair.

"Summerville," I said in surprise and pleasure.

I hadn't seen George Summerville since the Peninsular War. Summerville had been in a heavy cavalry regiment, a big man full of bonhomie, who'd made friends wherever he'd gone. I remembered long nights with him that involved much-flowing port but never how those nights had ended. Memories of the terrible headaches in the mornings, on the other hand, lingered. Summerville had been injured at Salamanca, and I'd lost track of him after that.

I advanced and held out my hand, shaking his warmly. "How are you, Lieutenant?"

"Lieutenant no longer. Sold my commission. You?"

"Half-pay." I'd gotten into the Army a roundabout way—volunteered, then obtained the rank of cornet with the help of my mentor. That's how poor gentlemen get to be officers. At Talavera, I'd been promoted from lieutenant to captain. Three years ago, I'd left the Peninsula in a devil's bargain with my aforementioned mentor, and now eked out a living in London.

"Lacey, allow me to introduce m' fiancee, Miss Lydia Wright. And her family. This is Captain Gabriel Lacey, a dashing dragoon of the Thirty-Fifth Light."

I made a bow, and Miss Wright and her parents greeted me politely. Miss Wright's red-blond hair was dressed in a simple knot, and she wore a high-waisted, modest gown and a dark wool spencer against the weather. She looked well turned out, neat, respectable.

There was nothing to object to in the Wrights, but they seemed rather lackluster for Summerville. Already they'd faded into the background while the boisterous Summerville commanded the light. Ever after I was unable to remember what Miss Wright's mother even looked like.

"I say, Lacey, a word in your ear?" Summerville put his hand on my shoulder and began to subtly but firmly turn me from the group. "Do you mind, Miss Wright? Won't be a moment."

Miss Wright seemed not to mind at all. She smiled, curtseyed to her fiancée, and remained within the safe circle of her parents. They turned collectively to examine jewelry the eager proprietor brought forth.

When we reached an empty corner of the shop, Summerville lowered his booming voice to a murmur. "I'm in a bit of a difficulty, Lacey. You see, I've lost something."

He looked worried. I'd never considered Summerville a good soldier, but he'd been excellent at keeping up the spirits of the rest of us. No night could be so dismal that Summerville could not warm it with his laughter and jests. Summerville worried was an unusual sight.

"Something valuable?" I asked when he hesitated.

"No, not exactly. But . . ." Summerville paused again, as though debating what to tell me. "I've heard you've become all the crack at ferreting out things. Mr. Grenville himself boasts of your cleverness."

"Does he?" I felt a bite of irritation. Lucius Grenville, the most famous dandy in England and now my friend, was apt to sing my praises a little too loudly, thus building expectations I could never hope to meet.

"He does, my old friend," Summerville said. "The thing is, I've mislaid my walking stick."

I leaned on my own walking stick, a gift from my

lady. He looked so anxious that I grew curious in spite of myself. "One of great importance to you?" Perhaps Miss Wright had given it to him.

"No, no. The bloody thing isn't worth much on its own. It does have a bit of gold on the head, but the main thing is, my name is engraved on it." He darted a glance at his companions, a very proper miss and her very proper parents, absorbed in studying the jewelry. "Look here, Lacey, I must find that walking stick. I might have left it in a dashed awkward place—a place I wouldn't want it coming to certain ears I'd visited, if you take my meaning."

I was beginning to understand. "Summerville, the reveler," I said. "You have not changed in that respect?"

"Those days are behind me, I assure you, except for a bit of an outing last night."

"Sowing the last of your wild oats?" I suggested.

He patted my shoulder, happy I'd caught on. "Exactly. I'd be ever so grateful if you could lay your hands on it for me. Today, I mean."

My irritation returned. "Today?"

"I know it much to ask, but the Wrights have my time well spoken for. I will not have a moment to scour London for it myself, and sooner or later one of them will ask what became of it. My peccadilloes are the past, but I had to go and lose that blasted stick. I would hate someone to try to touch me for money because of it. You understand?"

He looked so miserable that I stemmed my annoyance. Summerville's concern about blackmail was not farfetched. I put Mr. Wright as a well-off gentleman of the middle class, possibly a City man who had banks doing what he told them to do. Miss Wright was a catch, especially for a gentleman like Summerville, who had family connections but not much money.

In these desperate times, a lady of the demimonde might indeed threaten exposure to a gentleman due to come into means. Any whiff of scandal would make Mr. and Mrs. Wright whisk their debutante daughter far out of Summerville's reach.

"I understand," I said. "Tell me where you left it, and I'll fetch it for you." I'd find the stick and make Summerville promise to stay home from now on.

"That's dashed good of you," Summerville said, his good-natured smile returning. " Only . . . there are any number of places it might be."

"Any number? What the devil did you get up to last night, Summerville?"

He flushed. "Several things, as I recall." Quickly he told me the worrisome places he'd visited, and I noted them in my memory.

"The devil's own luck you found me today," I said.

"Not really. I called in at your rooms earlier, and your man told me where you'd be."

My valet had once been Grenville's footman, as pleased as his former master about my ability to find the un-findable. I scowled. "I will make the inquiries. For old times' sake."

"God bless you, Lacey." Summerville beamed like sudden sunshine.

He returned to his party with considerable cheer. Summerville chose a diamond bracelet for his blushing fiancée, then the foursome said their farewells and left the shop.

The proprietor returned to me less hopefully.

"I'll have this." I pointed to a slim gold chain that was a little longer than a bracelet. A tiny bell with a golden clapper dangled from it.

"Ah." The proprietor smiled at me, his interest awakened. "A most interesting choice, sir. A most interesting choice."

I DECIDED TO VISIT THE LAST NAME ON Summerville's list first.

I found the small house in Bishop's Lane, near Oxford Street, without mishap. The lane was so narrow that my hired hackney had to stop at the top of the street and let me down. I hobbled the rest of the way on my own in the rain, the tapping of my walking stick echoing from the close walls.

Number 20 was a tall, narrow house, with Doric columns flanking the front door and Greek pediments over the windows. A young footman opened the door and gazed haughtily down at me. I handed the impudent lad my card, upon which I'd scribbled that I'd come on behalf of Mr. Summerville.

The footman departed, closing the door in my face. He returned a short time after that, let me into the house, and commanded me to follow him.

He led me up a polished staircase to a back sitting room that overlooked a narrow garden. A cheerful fire crackled on the hearth, and low chairs with cushions invited lounging. Books that looked well used lay about on tables, and candles cut the gloom. It was the room of one who enjoyed comfort but not ostentation.

The lady in question entered. I stilled, finding myself enchanted.

Mrs. Chambers was a small woman with dark brown hair and blue eyes. Her turned-up nose gave her a young look, but the settled curves of her body put her in her early thirties.

She was not beautiful, but she was arresting, as comfortable and lovely as her private sitting room. Without saying a word, she made a gentleman want to linger here, made him long to sink back into her sofa's cushions and have her look at him with those eyes. I could only applaud Summerville's choice.

"Captain Lacey?" Mrs. Chambers held my card in her hand and polite inquiry in her tone.

I came straight to the point. "Mrs. Chambers, Mr. Summerville believes he left an article here last evening, and has sent me as an errand boy to fetch it."

Her smile bathed me in charm, and I decided that Summerville was a fool. He was choosing to marry the rather colorless Miss Wright instead of living out his days in comfort with this woman.

I knew why, of course. If Summerville wanted money and a career, Mrs. Chambers could give him neither. He would need the Wrights and their influence. Only the very rich or very poor could make a match in the demimonde without worry.

"A nasty day for such an errand," Mrs. Chambers said. "Please sit down, Captain. Would you like coffee? Or perhaps something against the damp?"

I took the armchair she indicated, noting that the cushions were, indeed, soft, and stretched my aching leg toward the fire. "I will not intrude upon you long. I will simply fetch the stick, if you have it, and go."

She sat in a smaller chair next to mine. I wondered whether I sat in Summerville's place, and she in the more ladylike chair next to it was the usual arrangement. If so, that arrangement was a cozy one.

"His walking stick?" she asked. "With the gold head?"

I nodded.

"I thought as much," she said. "He is always leaving it about."

I hoped she did have it. I would have liked nothing better than to sit in this friendly room and chat with the pleasant Mrs. Chambers instead of continuing my search in the cold rain. I'd remain here and return to Summerville later this afternoon.

"Why did he not simply call for it himself?" Mrs. Chambers asked. "Equally, he could have sent a note, rather than a friend loyal enough to soak himself in the attempt."

I returned a grateful smile and touched the top of my own walking stick. "I believe Mr. Summerville has pressing business, today. I was glad to oblige." That is, I had been regretting my hasty decision to help, but I was now much happier about it.

"You mean he is wooing the Wright girl," Mrs. Chambers said, her look turning wry. "Or rather, Miss Wright's father. You needn't worry, Captain. I know all about it."

She regarded me in amusement, and I felt sudden

impatience with Summerville. "I beg your pardon. I did not mean to embarrass you."

"I am not embarrassed in the least. I admit that I am not fond of his decision to marry, but I understand. Mr. Summerville hasn't many other avenues open to him."

"You are courageous," I said quietly.

Pain flashed in her eyes before her smile reappeared. Summerville leaving her to marry hurt her, I saw, but she had decided to put a brave face on it. I admired her for that.

"The walking stick?" I prompted.

"I'm afraid I do not remember him having it yesterday, though I will ask my footman."

Mrs. Chambers rose and rang a silver bell that rested on a tambour desk, and the lanky footman who'd admitted me entered the room.

"John," she said. "Did Mr. Summerville leave his walking stick behind last evening?"

John's face remained as expressionless as a blank wall. "I couldn't say, ma'am. Henry was on the door last night."

"I see. Thank you, John."

John bowed with trained stiffness and withdrew.

"Henry has gone to visit his family," Mrs. Chambers said once John had closed the door. "He'll not return for a few days. However, I will make inquiries of the other staff and have a good root around myself. If the walking stick turns up, I'll send it on to Mr. Summerville." She paused. "Or perhaps it would be more discreet if I sent it to you."

"That would be best," I answered, rising.

I took my card back from her and scribbled my direction on it: *Above Beltan's Bake Shop, Grimpen Lane, Covent Garden.*

"Thank you for seeing me, Mrs. Chambers," I said, handing her the card. "Your home is lovely."

Again, the flash of pain. "That is kind of you. Perhaps you would like to remain and take coffee?" She tried to look as though she'd love nothing better than for me to stay, but I saw in her eyes that she offered from simple politeness.

"I regret that I have another engagement." I did regret it. Sharply.

"Ah, well. I am pleased to have met you, Captain."

I confessed myself equally pleased, bowed, and took my leave.

THE RAIN WORSENED AS MORNING BECAME afternoon. I pulled my greatcoat around me and directed the hackney across London and down the river toward St. Katherine's Dock. Descending, I limped along the narrow lanes, conscious of scurrying feet in the shadows, of predators stalking unexpected prey.

I entered the lodgings Summerville had indicated, and a sharper contrast to Mrs. Chambers's comfortable house there was not. The stench of cabbage permeated the stairwell, and paint peeled from the walls. I climbed painfully to the second floor and knocked on the door at the top of the stairs.

A child cried fretfully within, and then I heard the unmistakable sound of a window being banged open.

The door was unlocked. I shoved myself inside in time to see a thin woman climbing over the windowsill. I crossed the room swiftly and grabbed her around the waist.

She screeched. "Lemme go!"

"You'll kill yourself, you little fool." I shoved her from me and slammed the casement closed.

She went for the door. Again, I caught her. She didn't weigh much, but she was strong.

"Stop!" I shook her. "I'm not a constable, whatever you may think."

She peered at me from behind a fall of yellow hair. "No? What are yer then?"

"I've come from Mr. Summerville." I glanced at the children on the floor. One was about four; the other, still crawling. Both of them had light brown hair the same shade as Summerville's.

"Oh. You mean our Dobbin."

I set her on her feet. "You are Nellie?"

"I am. Sorry I tried to fight yer. I though maybe you was coming for me." Nellie regarded me warily. "What'ya want, then?"

"Mr. Summ— er, Dobbin, believes he might have left behind his walking stick. A black stick with a gold head."

Interest lit her eyes. "Gold, was it?"

I knew then that the stick wasn't here. This girl would have sold it the moment she'd found it, and no wonder. The disappointment on her face when she shook her head was genuine. "Never saw it."

"He did not have it with him when he visited yesterday?"

"Naw. Mind you, 'e weren't 'ere long, and it were late."

"Ah, well. I apologize for disturbing you."

I took in the room before I went. The chimney smoked, the children sat sullenly, and Nellie looked as though she hadn't had a good meal in a fortnight. I fished inside my pocket and took out what few shillings I had to spare.

"Here." I pressed them to her hand. "For your trouble."

I turned to go. Behind me, she chuckled. "Yer a soft touch, ye are, sir."

From the other side of the door came the sound of drunken voices and the tramping of heavy feet. Nellie gasped. "Me 'usband!"

"You say nothing," I said. The situation was awkward, but not insurmountable. "I will speak to him."

The door banged open, and a man who must have weighed twenty stone filled the doorway. He was red faced, greasy haired, and cup-shot. Two men almost as large as he was crowded in behind him.

"Who the devil—"

Before her husband could say one word more, Nellie flew at me, screeching. "'E's a peach! Come about the money. Run for it!"

"Oh 'is 'e?" Nellie's husband reached for me.

I knew that Nellie acted out of self-preservation. For her husband to find her alone with an unknown gentleman only invited him to knock her about. I suspected he commonly did so, regardless. But as the large man and his equally large friends pounced on me, I could not feel much understanding.

Years battling the Corsican Monster in Spain and Portugal, and before that, service in India, had honed my skills, but I lagged against three huge men, and my ruined leg hindered me. They hauled me down the stairs, me fighting all the way, and tossed me into the street.

I landed, as luck would have it, on my bad leg. I lay groaning on the cobbles, cursing walking sticks in general and Summerville in particular.

I'd kept hold of my own walking stick, a fine weapon, but after traveling the length of London, spending too many precious coins, and being pummeled for my pains, I was no closer to finding Summerville's.

"Sir?" a gentle voice above me asked. "Can I help?"

I peered up through the rain to see a familiar face hovering over me. I'd seen the same face this morning in the jewelers' shop, but this apparition wore a threadbare coat, shabby clothes, and the dog collar of a parson.

"Summerville?"

AS THE MAN HELPED ME TO MY FEET, I REALIZED HE wasn't Summerville. At least, not *my* Summerville.

He walked me to the relative warmth of his rooms on the ground floor of a nearby boarding house and fed me coffee.

"I am vicar here, of this parish," Franklin Summerville told me as we sipped the rather weak brew. "There was never much money in the family. Most of it went to buy George his commission. George took the sword; I took the cloth."

I thought that the cloth had been rather thrust upon him, but I did not say so.

Realization struck me. "You are Dobbin," I said.

He stared at me, stricken. "Pardon?"

"You are the father of Nellie's children." I sat back, stretching my game leg. My coat was ripped, and my valet, Bartholomew, would be greatly distressed. He'd give my bruises as much attention, but Bartholomew prided himself on keeping my few garments fine. "I thought your brother to be her paramour at first. But he is not, is he?"

"What is your game, Captain? If you came here on George's behalf, do not waste your breath. I have nothing. And if he accosts Nellie again, I'll . . . Well, he will regret it."

I regarded him in surprise. "I do not go in for blackmail, sir. Do I take it that your brother does?"

Franklin's rage faded, and he shook his head. "I do not know why George expects that I'll give him money. He needs money, you know, to cover his gaming debts, of which there are always so many. Last night, when I refused to give him anything, he went to Nellie and tried to frighten her." Franklin shot me a smile. "My Nellie doesn't frighten so easily."

"So I noticed," I said dryly. After a moment I said, "You love her."

"God forgive me, but I do. Her husband is a brute,

and I can't . . ." He sighed. "I can only do for her what I can."

I rose. "Please give Nellie my best wishes."

He got to his feet with me. "But why did George send you to her? Not for money?"

"Your brother mislaid his walking stick. Did he leave it with you?"

"Walking stick? No. But I remember him having it. He waved it in my face. It had a gold head. And he was trying to touch *me* for money."

I nodded, believing him. "Thank you for your kindness, Mr. Summerville. It was much needed."

I took leave of him and hobbled away to find another hackney, my limp more pronounced than when I'd arrived.

I thought knew now where the walking stick was. I was half tempted to leave it there and fetch it tomorrow, after a bath and a long night's sleep, but I wanted to be finished with Summerville. I wanted to face Lady Breckenridge—the lady of blunt observations and bottomless blue eyes—without the distraction of him.

THE NEXT NAME THAT GRACED MY LIST WAS A gaming hell in St. James's Square called The Nines. The Nines was owned by a man called Bates and an aging courtesan by name of Mrs. Fuller. The house catered to the upper classes who strolled to it from White's and Brooks's, but in truth, it admitted anyone Bates thought might drop a sufficient amount of cash.

Men played against the house, and the house mostly won.

I'd been here before, with Grenville. I'd kept my bets modest and so had Grenville—modest for Grenville, that is—but we'd watched a young man lose seven thousand pounds on one throw of dice and be turned out of the house, ruined.

The doorman let me in from the darkening street without question and ushered me upstairs to Mr. Bates's private office. I knew that Bates admitted me and greeted me courteously not only because of my connection with Grenville but because of my growing connection with Viscountess Breckenridge. *Feet firmly under the table,* was a phrase I'd heard used about me. Bates was marking me as a person to fleece in future.

"I never saw Summerville with a walking stick," Bates said. Bates was such a tall, healthy-looking man that one would never imagine he spent most of his waking hours indoors, bent over gaming tables or counting money from said tables.

"With a gold head, you say?" he asked. "I'd have taken it from him if he'd brought such a thing. Summerville slipped out last night without paying what he owed—close to three hundred pounds it was. If he does not return with the money, I'll have the bailiffs on him."

The haze surrounding my memories of Summerville cleared still further, to remind me that Summerville had been good at losing money and equally skilled at touching others for more. He'd been ingenuous, warm, and laughing about it, but never once during those years had he paid the money back.

"Mr. Summerville is about to be married," I said. "To a young lady heiress. Perhaps he will pay his debts after that."

Bates gave me an aggrieved look. "Her father might not be foolish enough untangle the money for Mr. Summerville's use. Marriage settlements can be tricky. Please tell Mr. Summerville that if he continues to be careless, he'll spend his wedding night in the Fleet."

I thanked Bates for his time and took my leave. Outside, what light had touched the evening had gone, the rain poured down, and wind gusts sent the cold straight through me. I pulled my greatcoat closed against the weather and climbed into yet another hackney.

MY LIST BORE ONE MORE ADDRESS, AN EQUALLY notorious hell in Pall Mall, but I did not bother with it. I made my way back to number 20, Bishop's Lane, and presented my card to John when he opened the door. He took me upstairs right away, at least, and did not make me stand out in the rain.

I waited a full half hour before Mrs. Chambers entered her sitting room. She was dressed for the evening in a gray silk gown that bared her shoulders and much of her plump bosom. Wherever she intended to go, I predicted that she would eclipse every woman in the room.

"Captain?" She peered at my bruised face and torn coat in concern. "Are you well?"

"No." I made a formal bow. "Mrs. Chambers, I will just take the walking stick and go."

Her color rose. "Walking stick?"

"You have it, do you not?"

Mrs. Cambers gazed at me for a long moment, then she turned and rang the silver bell. In a few moments, a footman appeared—not John this time.

"Henry," Mrs. Chambers said. "Have Annie fetch Mr. Summerville's walking stick from my armoire, please."

Henry bowed and withdrew. I gathered that he truly hadn't gone to visit his family.

"How did you find me out?" Mrs. Chambers asked in the ensuing silence. She did not invite me to sit down again, nor did she offer me a beverage.

"You were not surprised when I told you what I'd come for," I said. "You had a glib explanation that Summerville always left the walking stick about, but I do not think he does. Summerville is careful even when he seems not to be, which is part of his charm, I think. And he was too worried when he found it missing to make me believe this a common occurrence. You questioned John, who would not have taken it at the door last night, instead of Henry who had. You did not want to make Henry lie."

Mrs. Chambers listened to my tale, her lips parting. When I finished, she looked away. "I had not planned to keep it. But when you turned up, saying he'd sent you, I realized how anxious Mr. Summerville was for the walking stick's discreet return. And I understood what that meant."

That Summerville had realized the danger of

having the walking stick found in the house of his mistress. The utterly respectable Wrights would never forgive the transgression. Summerville also believed Mrs. Chambers might try to blackmail him with it, which put plainly just how much trust he had in her. And so Mrs. Chambers had decided to act.

I looked into Mrs. Chambers' clear eyes and suddenly wished myself a wealthy man, so I could press money to her palm and tell her to go somewhere, anywhere, to forget about Summerville and pursue her own happiness.

"I am sorry," I said. I truly was sorry. Sorry I'd ever agreed to help Summerville.

"The *ton* can gossip all they like that he is my protector," she said, "but such talk can be dismissed as gossip." *Especially by Summerville, the charmer.* "But the stick is proof, isn't it? Proof I can show to his beloved fiancée and her father."

I studied her brittle face, her too-bright eyes. "You love him?"

"Yes. I am afraid that I do."

"He does not deserve you," I said savagely.

She smiled, but the smile was strained. "You are kind, Captain. But it does not matter. I told you this morning that I understand why he must marry. And I do. Marriages should not be made lightly."

"But you do mind."

"Of course I mind! Do you think I have no heart? He must lie in a bed with her and get children on her, and for that I want to gouge her eyes out!" Her rage faded as abruptly as it had come, and she gave a little laugh. "You see, Captain? I am petty and jealous, as is any woman who wants a gentleman."

I took a step forward. "You are brave. I wish . . ." I stopped. "I am friends with Mr. Grenville, who has a large acquaintance. Perhaps he could introduce you to a gentleman who proves more appreciative than Summerville."

She was shaking her head before I finished. "No. I know you mean it as kindness, Captain, but no."

"I wish you were not so in love with him," I said.

She shook her head again. We watched each other, the words hanging.

Henry entered at this interesting moment, carrying a black walking stick with a gold head. Mrs. Chambers took it from him, dismissed him, and put the walking stick into my hands.

"There, Captain. Tell Mr. Summerville not to be so careless with it in future."

I bowed again, but I had no more words to give her.

My coming had hurt her. If Summerville had not sent me, certain Mrs. Chambers presented a threat, she might never have realized how much he mistrusted her, how much he viewed her as an embarrassment. I'd sown a seed of darkness.

"Good-bye," I said, and left her.

When I reached Summerville's rooms in Piccadilly, his valet was dressing him to go out. Summerville turned from the mirror, his expression hopeful. He did not even inquire about my bruises. "Did you find it?"

I looked him over, from the elaborate cravat his valet had just tied to the pristine pumps he wore with pantaloons that buttoned at the ankle. I thought of his brother, the threadbare parson, and Nellie in her tiny rooms with her children and her drunken husband. I thought of lovely Mrs. Chambers and the misery in her eyes, misery Summerville had put there.

"Yes," I said.

Summerville's smile flashed. "Thank God. I knew you'd do it. Grenville said you were astonishing. Where is it?"

"In a safe place." I had stopped at Grosvenor Street and given it to Grenville's very discreet valet to look after.

His smile faded. "Have you not brought it with you?"

I glanced meaningfully at the valet, and Summerville took the hint. "Leave us, Waters." The valet bowed and departed.

"What are you playing at, Lacey? Where did you find it?"

I ignored his questions, letting my temper rise. "I toyed with the idea of returning it to you—end-first with you bent over, but I decided that would not be practical."

Summerville flushed. "I do not find that amusing, Lacey."

"It was not meant to be. Instead, I decided to ask you to make out a draft for one hundred pounds."

"One hundred—" Summerville gaped. "You are

joking. Why the devil do you want a hundred pounds?"

"Fifty of it I will give to Nellie, because she has need of it. The other fifty I will give to Mrs. Chambers for putting up with you. The three hundred you owe to The Nines is between you and Mr. Bates."

A muscle moved in his jaw. "Very well. I suppose you've put yourself out for me today. I will give you your one hundred pounds. A fee, shall we say? For locating the walking stick."

He insulted me. A gentleman did not fetch and carry for money. I did not react to his suggestion, and Summerville gave up and strode to his writing table. Candlelight shone on his immaculate white neckcloth as he sat down, sharpened a pen, and dipped it into his ink pot. He wrote hastily, the scratching of the pen loud in the stillness.

"There." He snatched up the paper and nearly threw it at me.

I took the bank draft, examined it, and tucked it into my pocket.

"Thank you. Next month, I will return, and you will write another draft, for the same purpose. And the next month after that."

"The devil I will. My income is not substantial, Lacey."

"Better marry your Miss Wright quickly then."

Summerville slammed himself up from the chair. "You go too far, Lacey. How dare you?"

I eyed him coldly, our heights nearly the same. "If I do not receive the sum of one hundred pounds from you at the first of each month, to be dispersed as I've outlined, your walking stick will turn up somewhere far more embarrassing than in the houses of Mrs. Chambers or your brother's paramour. I know people in many places, Summerville. You would do well not to have your name associated with them."

Summerville stared in disbelief, then he snarled and lunged at me.

My sword flashed out of my cane. Summerville stopped, looking down at the point of my blade resting against his immaculate cravat.

"Stand at ease, Lieutenant," I said quietly. "Or do you want to ruin your suit?"

"Blast you, Lacey. You're nobody. You always were nobody. How dare you?"

"I am a gentleman of the Thirty-Fifth Light," I said. "Who are you?"

"I am a gentleman who will have the power to ruin you in a few years' time."

I made a frosty bow. "Then for a few years at least, you will do some good by these ladies." I sheathed the sword. "Good night, Mr. Summerville."

I left him cursing as I walked out of the room and hobbled back down the stairs and into the rain.

The next afternoon, I found Lady Breckenridge at Lady Aline Carrington's garden party, as I had known I would. The rain had gone, and the sun shone at last, chased away from time to time by a breath of cloud.

"There you are, Gabriel," Donata Breckenridge

said as I walked to her. "Thank God. Sir Neville Percy has been following me about in attempt to engage me in conversation, and he is so very bad at it. Pretty to look at is Sir Neville, but a ghastly bore. He ought to stand under an arch for full effect and keep his mouth closed."

"I am pleased to be of some use to you," I said, making a bow.

"Do not be sardonic, Lacey; it doesn't suit you. Leave the mockery to me." She smiled as she spoke, a genuine smile, and warmth stole through the chill I'd carried since leaving Mrs. Chambers's house the evening before.

"I have something for you," I said.

"Truly?" Lady Breckenridge forgot all about Sir Neville and turned her full attention to me.

I slipped a small parcel from my pocket and handed it to her. Lady Breckenridge peeled back the cloth in which I'd wrapped the gift, and gazed in some surprise at the gold chain with its tiny bell that lay on the piece of blue velvet.

I leaned down and murmured into her ear. "For your ankle."

The look Donata Breckenridge gave me said that she did not find me as old or weary as I felt. She turned and strolled away from me, giving me a little smile over her shoulder.

I caught up to her under the shadows of the ivy, where she stopped and raised her lips to mine.

A NOTE FROM THE AUTHOR

I hope you enjoyed this collection of shorter works in Captain Lacey's saga.

The Necklace Affair started off as a short story, written to keep myself entertained (and sane) while I waited eight hours in a jury room to see whether I'd be called (I was not). The story remained unpublished, forgotten in a file on my computers for years. When I began republishing the Captain Lacey series, I found it, rewrote it as a longer novella, and fit it between *The Sudbury School Murders* and *A Body in Berkeley Square*.

The Gentleman's Walking Stick was a story I'd submitted to a contest run by a small press for inclusion in a Regency anthology. I had submitted another story (a romance), and both were the highest scoring entries in the contest. However, they could only include one in the printed anthology, so they chose the romance, and published *The Gentleman's Walking Stick* in an online magazine that has since vanished. This was one of the first stories I'd penned about Captain Lacey.

I revised it a bit to fit the timeline of the novels of the series, the story falling somewhere after the events of *A Body in Berkeley Square*.

The Disappearance of Miss Sarah Oswald was the very first Captain Lacey story I wrote. I submitted it to a small print magazine where it was purchased and published. It went on to be nominated for an award called the Derringer by a mystery short story writers and readers organization. The reception of this story encouraged me to try writing a longer book about Captain Lacey, which resulted in *The Hanover Square Affair*.

Thank you so much for reading! For more information on the Captain Lacey series, visit my website at www.gardnermysteries.com. There you can also subscribe to my newsletter, which is sent out to announce new book releases.

Thank you again!

Best wishes,

Ashley Gardner

ALSO BY ASHLEY GARDNER

Captain Lacey Regency Mystery Series
The Hanover Square Affair
A Regimental Murder
The Glass House
The Sudbury School Murders
The Necklace Affair
A Body in Berkeley Square
A Covent Garden Mystery
A Death in Norfolk
A Disappearance in Drury Lane
Murder in Grosvenor Square
The Thames River Murders
The Alexandria Affair
A Mystery at Carlton House
Murder in St. Giles
Death at Brighton Pavilion

The Gentleman's Walking Stick
(short stories: in print in
The Necklace Affair and Other Stories)

Kat Holloway "Below Stairs" Victorian Mysteries
(writing as Jennifer Ashley)
A Soupçon of Poison
Death Below Stairs
Scandal Above Stairs
Death in Kew Gardens

Leonidas the Gladiator Mysteries
(writing as Ashley Gardner)
Blood Debts
(More to come)

Mystery Anthologies
Past Crimes

ABOUT THE AUTHOR

USA Today Bestselling author Ashley Gardner is a pseudonym for *New York Times* bestselling author Jennifer Ashley. Under both names—and a third, Allyson James—Ashley has written more than 85 published novels and novellas in mystery and romance. Her books have won several *RT BookReviews* Reviewers Choice awards (including Best Historical Mystery for *The Sudbury School Murders*), and Romance Writers of America's RITA (given for the best romance novels and novellas of the year). Ashley's books have been translated into more than a dozen different languages and have earned starred reviews in *Booklist*. When she isn't writing, she indulges her love for history by researching and building miniature houses and furniture from many periods.

More about the Captain Lacey series can be found at the website: www.gardnermysteries.com.

Stay up to date on new releases by joining her email alerts here: http://eepurl.com/5n7rz

CPSIA information can be obtained
at www.ICGtesting.com
Printed in the USA
LVHW091530050219
606471LV00003B/530/P

9 781946 455468